FALLING FOR A STAR

Thea loves her job in TV, but hates her boss Hermione. When Thea gets a chance to interview her favourite movie star, Justin Anderson, Hermione is willing to do anything to sabotage the blossoming romance between her underling and the handsome actor. Then Thea gets the chance to stay in Justin's country mansion and do some in-depth research. But is he really as nice as he seems? And will she become just another one of his easy conquests?

PATRICIA KEYSON

◆

FALLING FOR A STAR

Complete and Unabridged

LINFORD
Leicester

First published in Great Britain in 2015

First Linford Edition
published 2018

A catalogue record for this book is available
from the British Library.

ISBN 978–1–4448–3579–3

Published by
F. A. Thorpe (Publishing)
Anstey, Leicestershire

Set by Words & Graphics Ltd.
Anstey, Leicestershire
Printed and bound in Great Britain by
T. J. International Ltd., Padstow, Cornwall

This book is printed on acid-free paper

1

Thea looked at the image on the television monitors in front of her. Justin Anderson was a megastar, and although his good looks weren't lost on her, they weren't her main concern at that moment. Ideas buzzed around her head as she went through possible scenarios for an interview with him. If only she'd been asked to do it! What an impossible thought that was. She'd only been working at the TV production company for a short time, and was very much a junior in the celebrity documentaries and popular interest section. Through the headphones she listened intently to what was being said by the interviewer. They weren't the sort of questions Thea felt excited about.

Long after his image disappeared, Thea's gaze remained on the monitors as she thought about Justin Anderson. Then she became aware of someone enquiring in an acid tone, 'Thea, where are those files I need?'

Bringing herself back from her dream world to the present, Thea stammered, 'I'm sorry, Hermione,' before slipping the armful of papers onto her line manager's desk.

'For goodness' sake, get a grip,' commanded Hermione Clutterbuck. 'He's a here-today-gone-tomorrow sort. I should know, I've seen enough of them.'

'Of course you have, Hermione, you've been here since the year dot,' the boss said, approaching them and winking in Thea's direction. 'As Hermione appears to have a deskful of work, I'd like your help please, Thea. Come.' He strode out towards his office with Thea trailing behind him.

'Sit down, Thea,' invited Dave. 'I'd like to see you having more responsibility. Do you think you could handle it?'

'Definitely,' Thea assured him. She

hoped she looked ready to take on an assignment.

'An interview? Think you could manage?'

'Oh yes, no problem.' Thea wondered if she might be sent to interview a sportsperson, or maybe a politician. She leaned forward, trying not to look as eager as she felt. 'Who's it to be?' she asked nonchalantly.

'Justin Anderson.'

Thea's gasp of breath was plainly audible. She tried to cover her shock by saying, 'But he's already been interviewed. There was a row of screens showing him just two minutes ago.' What was going on? Was he testing her? She couldn't understand it.

'Sure — and have you watched the interview?'

Thea kept her eyes on him. 'Yes . . . ' She hoped she wouldn't have to comment on it and be unprofessionally backstabbing against a colleague.

'It's difficult for me to admit this, and I don't want to be disloyal, but I'm sure you'll keep this confidential.' He paused as Thea nodded. 'Truth is, Hermione drew up the questions that Justin was answering. You've seen the footage, eh?' Thea nodded again. 'Well,' continued Dave, 'they're not really very probing questions — just the usual superficial ones about his films, his good looks, and his girlfriends. We can't use Hermione's interview.'

Thea was surprised he was being so critical of his top presenter, although she understood the point he was making. 'You want something about his life outside of his celebrity bubble?'

'Exactly,' breathed Dave. 'You're bright; knew you'd catch on. Right, I'll leave it to you, then.'

'But won't Hermione mind?' Thea was incredulous; Hermione Clutterbuck was a very egotistical sort of person. Thea knew she could create all sorts of difficulties for her if she didn't like what was going on.

'Oh, yes, Thea, she'll mind. Very much. Hermione doesn't like to be outdone. You'll have to watch your back. Well, do you want the job or not?'

'I want it, please,' said Thea, standing up, eager to plan her campaign.

Thea sat in her allocated corner with a block of paper and a biro, jotting things down in a spider diagram. In between working out her questions, she dealt with phone calls, ran for files, answered emails and wondered how she was going to keep things secret from Hermione.

'Here, take these reviews and put them on the website.'

'Yes, Hermione.'

'What did Dave want with you? Been caught with your hand in the till?' Hermione twitched a smile from her mean mouth.

Thea wondered why she had to be so unkind. 'No, nothing like that,' she told her. This was getting a bit too close for comfort, but she'd promised Dave she'd be discreet. Trying to be tactful, Thea added, 'I like your new picture on the website; there have been a lot of comments admiring it.'

'Have there?' Hermione preened like a peacock. 'I'll have a look sometime.'

The way she rushed back to her desk and frantically clicked the mouse amused Thea. She breathed a sigh of relief and allowed herself a smile. By the time she was due to finish her shift she'd got a good stack of questions for Justin Anderson. She had also made a list of film titles and reviews which she had transferred to her laptop.

★   ★   ★

Thea stepped out into the evening, feeling the air fresh on her face and excitement bubbling inside her. The sunshine suited her mood and she could feel the spring in her step as she bounced along. This was just so great; not only was she doing a job she enjoyed, she had an interview with Justin Anderson to look forward to. Even the difficulties she was having with Hermione faded into insignificance. Dave was the boss and he trusted her to do a good job. Away from the hawk-like gaze of Hermione, she allowed herself a few minutes to wonder how the interview would proceed and where it would take place. Deciding to walk home for once, Thea crossed the road, questions rolling around her head.

The next thing she knew, she was on the ground with a nasty ache in her left arm, which was trapped underneath her. Lying with her eyes shut, Thea was aware of traffic noises, and knew she should make an effort to get out of the road, but she couldn't move. Shock rooted her to the spot. With her eyes closed, her hearing became more dominant and, along with the rush of cars and lorries, she heard several voices, recognising none of them.

'Don't move her,' someone commanded.

'Is she dead?' asked a young voice.

'It's all right, she's breathing and I think she's conscious.'

Now, that voice she *did* recognise. Struggling to focus, she stared up into the face she knew well, mesmerised by the soft grey-green gaze of his eyes. He bent down close to her and asked, 'How are you feeling?'

'I'm fine.' Thea smiled. 'What happened?'

'You crossed the road without looking and something was coming. Not a wise move.'

Thea struggled into a more ladylike position, glad she was wearing trousers and not a skirt. 'What hit me? Was it a ten-ton lorry?'

A gentle chuckle was followed by, 'Not quite. It was a schoolboy on his bike.'

'Is he all right?' Thea was mortified. She desperately hoped she hadn't hurt a child.

'He's fine. It's you I'm worried about.'

Although Thea wouldn't have wished this situation on anyone, she was quite pleased that she'd ended up in the middle of the road with Justin Anderson worrying about her. She could hardly believe it was him. Was she concussed and imagining it?

'If you think you can move, we'll continue this conversation on the pavement. What do you say?'

Strong arms helped Thea out of further harm's way and someone from a coffee shop brought a chair for her to sit on. Blinking, just to make sure she wasn't seeing things, Thea said, 'It *is* you. I thought I recognised your voice.'

He beckoned to a child wearing a cycle helmet.

Thea felt awful. 'I'm sorry. I should have looked where I was going. My mind was elsewhere. Did I frighten you?'

'I'm sorry too,' the boy said, reddening slightly. 'I was texting. Are you okay?'

'I'm fine. Are *you* hurt?'

'No, I'm all right. I wasn't going fast.' With a puzzled expression he gazed at

Justin. 'Do I know you? You look like someone. You're Justin Anderson!'

Justin grinned at him. 'That's me.'

'My big sister likes you.' The boy reddened still further. 'She's got posters of you on her walls and she's seen all your films. I think they're bor — '

Justin laughed. 'Is your bike damaged at all?' he asked.

'The chain's come off, but it's okay.'

'I'll fix that,' offered Justin, kneeling on the pavement to inspect the greasy chain. The boy glanced at Thea, and she winked to reassure him that it was just fine for Justin Anderson to mend his bike. Although she was feeling as awestruck as the boy looked.

'Thanks,' said the boy when Justin had finished repairing the bike. He turned to Thea. 'I'm glad I didn't kill you or put you in hospital.'

'Me too,' she said, smiling, although there were definite benefits to being knocked down by a bike if Justin Anderson came to your rescue.

'Would you like my autograph, even

if it's just to prove to your sister that you really met me?' Justin took a notebook from his jacket pocket.

The boy nodded enthusiastically, took the signature and pedalled off.

'Now, how are you feeling?' Justin asked her.

Lightheaded; crazy about you; like the luckiest girl in the world. She must be in shock to be reduced to this gibbering wreck of a woman. Nevertheless, she couldn't believe she was sitting next to Justin Anderson. He was chatting to her as though he'd known her for ages. It might be a good time to ask about the interview now he was within her grasp, so to speak. On the other hand, perhaps it wasn't very professional to turn a road traffic accident into an opportunity which he might suspect had been engineered.

Aware of an expectant silence, she realised he was waiting for an answer. 'Never better,' she said.

In reality, her arm ached like hell, but she didn't think it was broken. In order to take advantage of her time with Justin, she looked at him. Up close he was even more gorgeous than on screen. At the moment, he looked like Izaak Flanagan, the hero he played in his latest film. Apart from a smear of bike grease across his cheek, his face was perfect. She watched in amazement as his grubby hand moved towards her and gently stroked her hair.

2

Suddenly, he pulled away from her. 'I'm sorry, I forgot; I'm covered in oil. You've grazed your forehead, but I think the bleeding's stopped now; I was just making sure.' He reached into his jacket pocket, brought out a large clean tissue, and dabbed at her face. He inspected her and treated her to a full smile. In all the pictures that Thea had seen of him, he had a dark, brooding look, sometimes a half-smile, but never anything like this. As her hand went to her head to try and steady her feelings, Justin's face fell. 'You're hurting more than you're letting on. Where were you heading when you walked into the bike?'

'Home. And you?' She was beginning to wonder if she'd had a bad bump on the head. Why else would she have the cheek to ask Justin Anderson where he was going?

'I'm meeting some friends, but I've been at the studio. It's in this area. Anything else you'd like to know?' he asked, grinning at her. She shook her head. 'Right then, I think I'd better take you home.' He raised his arm to hail a taxi.

Justin Anderson was about to take her home. Life couldn't get any better, but it could definitely get worse. Hermione was striding out of the office building and heading straight towards them. Her strident tones hit Thea with more force than the bicycle. 'What have you done now?' she asked dismissively. Turning on the charm, she said, 'Justin, how delightful. I'm so sorry if this young lady has been causing you any problems. She's our office junior. I'm afraid she won't last long in the cut and thrust of the television world.'

'Henrietta, isn't it? You interviewed me.'

Hermione's mouth curved downwards. 'Hermione, Hermione Clutterbuck. I'll take over now. We don't want you wasting your time with . . . ' She waved her hand vaguely in Thea's direction.

'I'm not sure what to do. I don't really want to be late, but I would like to make sure she gets home all right and is as well as she says. She might have bumped her head quite severely.' He looked anxiously at Thea, who smiled weakly, hoping he would insist on taking her home.

'No, no, I'm sure it's nothing serious. She's always like this. Don't you worry. As I said, you've got better things to do than worry about office girls. I'll deal with her.'

Indecision flitted across Justin's face, but with a quick look at his watch, he appeared to give in. 'I hope you'll be okay,' he said to Thea, and with a 'Bye, Henrietta' he hopped into the taxi which had been waiting.

Hermione hailed another taxi, bundled Thea into it, told her she'd better be at work the next day, and marched off towards the tube station.

* * *

Back at her flat, Thea made a cup of tea, then settled on the comfy sofa and closed her eyes. If only Hermione hadn't turned up, she would have been here with Justin. Thea wondered why the older woman had been so uncaring about the accident, and why she'd dismissed Justin with such determination. Putting those thoughts from her head, Thea began to daydream. As Justin's lips were about to join hers in a wonderfully tender kiss, she spilt hot tea on her leg and opened her eyes with a start.

She put her tea down and stretched out across the sofa, not even bothering to kick off her sandals. Her eyes drooped again. Once more she was transported to dreamland, where an earnest Izaak Flanagan had saved her from an outlandish devil-figure and was carrying her tenderly homeward. Izaak deposited her at her flat and departed to right more wrongs.

Reality kicked in. Justin was a celebrity, and people wanted to know more about him; she was the one who had been asked to find out his innermost thoughts. Oh, no! Thea strived to sit upright, wincing as she moved her arm. What would Justin Anderson think when the office trainee contacted him and asked for an interview? Looking back, she remembered he didn't know her name, so arranging the interview might not be a problem. And maybe he somehow wouldn't recognise her as the same person who had stupidly walked in front of a bike.

Even though it was still only early evening, Thea stripped off her clothes and threw them towards the washing machine, grabbed her bathrobe and a couple of painkillers and headed for the bath. Her head was now thumping.

The water soothed her a little, and after towelling herself dry, she heated some milk, remembering how her mother had looked after her when she felt unwell as a youngster. Hunting around for her handbag, which she couldn't even remember bringing home, Thea found it on the table, a place she'd never have put it normally. In one of the outer pockets she found a crumpled bit of paper torn from a notebook. She smoothed it out with her hand and made out a phone number and the letters 'JA'. No message, just his initials and the number. All she had to do was phone that number and ask Justin if he'd let her interview him. Simple, easy, straightforward. So what was wrong with the plan? She thought for a while and then answered herself: nothing. Even her headache started to recede as she called the number. Her head was thumping again as the dialling tone cut to a disembodied voice asking her to leave a message. She didn't want to. She needed to speak to him in person. She'd try again in the morning, but now she could do with an early night. Yawning widely, she settled into bed.

She slept fitfully, disturbed by wild dreams of Justin.

* * *

Thea was almost late for work for the first time. The thought of Hermione's acerbic tone had her running the last few hundred yards from the tube station and gasping up the stairs, too panicked to wait for the lift. She froze like a deer caught in headlights as Dave greeted her.

'Hi, Thea,' was all he said, nothing about lateness or enquiring if she'd arranged the interview yet. He was a great boss.

'Good afternoon, Thea. So good of you to join us,' said Hermione when Thea got to her desk and unloaded her bag.

Unable to think of a fitting reply without being rude, Thea just set to work.

'I've sent you an email with a list of links to various websites to trawl through. And I've forwarded queries which need answering this morning. And there's a message for you, I believe.' Hermione sniffed.

Thea's heart fluttered. It must be Justin. But why would Justin Anderson get in touch with her? And Hermione would hardly pass on something from him. 'Thank you,' Thea said, not wanting to sound too eager or play games with Hermione. She just waited, jotting down things on her block of paper for the, hopefully, upcoming interview.

'Don't you want to know what it's about?'

'I expect you'll tell me when you're ready,' replied Thea. 'I'm going to get a coffee from the machine, would you like one?'

Hermione's mouth worked, but no sound came. Eventually she managed to squeeze out, 'All right.'

When Thea returned with the two plastic cups of coffee, Hermione said, 'It's about the holiday rota. Dave wants it sorted out. Apparently you haven't put your name down for any time off.'

There were two reasons for that: Thea hadn't thought she'd still be in the job for long enough to qualify for leave; and anyway, if she *was* allowed to stay after her probationary period, she couldn't think of anywhere she'd rather be than at work. From what Dave had said yesterday, he valued her enough to keep her on. Now, with the thought of an interview with Justin, perhaps it would be a good idea to book some time away from the office if only to avoid Hermione's questioning about what she was doing. 'I haven't given it much thought. How long am I allowed?'

'Goodness me, I have no idea. *I'm* not an office girl. Go and see admin.'

Thea suppressed a smile. She wondered what had happened to Hermione to make her so mean and unapproachable. She was a good-looking woman, always immaculately made up, and dressed stylishly. No one would call her past it — no one would dare! She was pretty good at what she did, although Thea agreed with Dave about Hermione's interviewing techniques. No deep probing from her, just sensationalising. If Hermione put her mind to it she could be at the top of the media world. Thea spent a few minutes speculating as to whether some dark secret overshadowed Hermione's past. She'd probably just grown used to an easy life and couldn't be bothered to keep striving to learn new approaches. But, as Thea reminded herself, to dig deeply into a person's life, you had to research extensively, which was what she should be doing right now.

* * *

At lunchtime, Thea went into the tiny garden at the back of the offices and called Justin. This time he answered on the third ring.

'Justin, hello. My name's Thea Stafford and I'm a production assistant with FPC, the Filbert Production Company. We're commissioned to make topical inserts for a daily television programme, as well as documentaries and exposés. We'd like to conduct an in-depth interview and I wondered if I could arrange an initial meeting with you.' Silence followed. Thea gulped, this was difficult. There was still no reply. 'Justin? Are you there?'

'I've just been interviewed by them. By some hatchet-faced woman called Henrietta.'

Thea couldn't help but giggle, especially as Hermione had just opened the door onto the garden, hardly waiting to get outside before lighting up her foul cigarette. Hermione didn't do the polite thing of sitting at the other end of the garden and pretending to be interested in the flowers. Oh no, she came and perched on a chair right near Thea, flashing her an evil smile as she did so.

'Not in your way, am I?' she said.

Thea turned her back and whispered

into the phone, knowing Hermione would still be able to hear what she was saying, 'The phone's breaking up. I'll try again later.'

'Odd, I can hear you perfectly well. Okay, ring me back later. Thea, you say. Nice name.'

Thea felt herself blushing at his compliment. She hung up, put her phone back in her bag and turned to Hermione. 'Nice out here, isn't it? Enjoy your smoke.' There were several things she could have added, such as hoping the cigarettes would kill her, what would her online fans think if they had a picture of that on the site, et cetera, et cetera, but Thea was too kind to be that mean to Hermione. Instead, she disappeared inside again and went back to her desk.

There was no one around. Thea pulled out her mobile and called Justin again.

'Hello, Thea.' This time his voice was warm and alluring.

'Justin, hello again. It's Thea.' She

cringed as she realised her clumsiness.

'As I just said I was interviewed by your company recently. Why repeat the exercise?'

'Dave, my boss, had something more in-depth in mind. Hermione's version — very rightly, of course — dwelt on your films and your . . . good looks.' Thea's voice was starting to squeak. She covered the mouthpiece and coughed. 'Could you bear for me to interview you again and let our viewers find out about the real Justin Anderson?'

'You're welcome to try. Introduce me to him if you find him.'

'Great. Thanks. When would be good for you?'

They fixed a time and place and Thea set the phone down on her desk. She couldn't stop a smile settling on her face. Another meeting with Justin Anderson was really cool. For the moment she forgot that it might make her reputation in the media world, all she could see was herself and Justin enjoying quality time together. She would enchant him with her witty repartee, and he would declare her the most interesting person on the planet, swearing his allegiance to her for all eternity. But the reality was that her hands were slippery with sweat, and as she wiped them on her jeans, Hermione came back into the room and proceeded to nag her.

'Have you been in touch with admin? They won't hold over your days, you know.'

It took Thea a while to understand what she meant. Then the penny dropped. 'Anyone would think you want me out of the way,' she grinned. 'I'm off to see them now.'

Thea was surprised to find out that she was due two weeks of holiday. She took out her diary and looked through the empty pages. There was the interview with Justin to be considered now. If she took time off before it, she could do her research without having the interruption of other work-related tasks. What she'd do with the time afterwards, she had no idea. What a sad life she must have if her only thrills were from work. She rapidly selected the dates she wanted off and went to see Dave.

'I'm interviewing Justin Anderson during the first week of my leave. It'll give me time to do thorough research, do the interview and not put my foot in it in front of Hermione while I'm at it.'

Dave's face lit up. 'Good. You'll be working for the first week, so you'll get full pay. And you'll still be entitled to those days off. Also, I can afford a small allowance for entertaining, travel and suchlike.'

'I wasn't angling for any of that, I was only really letting you know that I'd been in touch with Justin.'

'Just being fair.'

'You're more than fair. I love working here with you.'

'But not Hermione, eh?' Dave gave a throaty laugh.

'I didn't say that,' murmured Thea,

bouncing her way back to the office.

'I've booked my leave,' she told Hermione, 'will you get someone from another department to help?' Thea had no idea how holiday was covered.

'No, I don't think so,' smiled Hermione, dangerously. 'We'll manage perfectly well without you I'm sure and don't forget the company is looking for ways to cut costs. So let's see how things go, shall we?'

Thea hadn't thought of that possibility. It looked as though there would be no job to come back to if Hermione got her way, and then what would she do?

3

Thea stood outside the station looking up and down the road. She had no idea what sort of vehicle would be picking her up or even if it would be Justin himself. They'd arranged to meet here at ten, and the station clock was already nudging its way to twenty past. Although Thea was quite a punctual person herself, preferring to be early rather than risk being late, she was happy to make allowances for Justin Anderson. Not quite sure how the day would turn out, Thea had made a mental note that they could get to The Ritz quite easily, or somewhere posh overlooking the river. With that in mind, she'd packed a couple of suitable outfits in a small case along with a change of underwear, in the probably vain hope that the day would turn into an evening. Her brief was to outline the interview about Justin and then Dave would organise the filming schedule when the time came. She hoped the questions she'd drawn up would give the viewers an insight into what Justin was really like.

The clock passed the half-hour and Thea shifted from foot to foot. Glancing down at her trainers, she once again admired their strawberry colour and the way they made her large feet look smaller. She hadn't had much opportunity to wear them. Today, however, seemed just perfect. A car honked, making her jump, and the rest of the people by the station look up disapprovingly. The car pulled in beside her and a young man was by her side in seconds.

'Yo, you Thea?' In answer to Thea's nod, he said, 'Hop in, ma'am, I'm Toby and I'm gonna take you to Justin.'

Thea hesitated. It was highly unlikely that anyone else would know she was meeting Justin here at this time, but she didn't fancy being kidnapped. She reached for her phone to call Justin. Toby loaded her case into the boot of the car and stood with the car door open, waiting for her to get in.

'I'm just checking something,' mumbled Thea.

'Yes, ma'am. Check all you like.' He grinned.

Justin's voicemail cut in. Dithering over whether to say something or not, she decided to front it out. 'Good, good, that's fine then. Thanks, Justin. See you soon,' she said, after finishing the call. She risked a covert glance at Toby, who was still grinning inanely. What if he were a mad axeman on the loose? Justin *must* have sent him. He was a chauffeur even if he didn't fit Thea's idea of one. She'd thought a uniform and peaked cap were obligatory, but Justin obviously didn't mind if his staff dressed in jeans and a torn t-shirt. Toby looked safe enough, and if she hesitated any longer he might drive off without her. She decided to chance it.

She slid into the rear of the car, which by now she'd seen for what it was: a stretch limo. As Toby eased into the traffic, she looked around the opulent surroundings. If she wanted music, it was there; if she wanted a cocktail, it was there; if she wanted to watch the telly, it was there. Wow, she thought, this is better than my little flat. I could move into this car and live well.

Assuming they would only be driving a short distance, Thea was concerned when the car hit the open road and revved up out of town. She wanted to ask Toby where they were going, but she had no idea how to communicate with him. In the end, she tried to catch his eye in the rear-view mirror and then knocked on the glass separating the front from the back.

'Yes, ma'am,' he called, his eyes still on the road. He pressed a switch and the glass retracted.

'For a start, please call me Thea.'

'Sure, ma'am, will do.'

'Where are we going?'

'To Justin's place. He said to bring you there.' Toby smoothly changed gear and overtook a sports car. 'By the way, ma'am, Justin's not on the end of his phone right now, he's on his way to meet us.' Toby chuckled and Thea felt herself blushing at being caught out. Telling herself that she'd have to be on her toes if she was to make a good impression on Toby and his boss, she sat up straight and tried to look composed.

Things seemed genuine; she may as well sit back and enjoy the ride. Toby was a good driver and Thea felt safe. She thought ahead to her meeting with Justin. As she tried to recall his face, she found it didn't appear clearly to her, which was silly as she'd seen him so often on the big screen as well as on billboards. Sighing, she recalled his nearness to her when she'd been run over. The smell of him was something she wouldn't forget; it was a distinctly clean fragrance as if he'd just stepped out from a soapy hot shower. She shivered at the thought.

The car stopped and Toby whistled as he came around to open her door. 'Here we are, ma'am. I'll just get your bag.'

After trying to get out of the car elegantly, she grabbed the handle of her bag and turned to thank Toby, but the car roared off, giving her no chance.

Looking around, she thought she'd been abandoned in the middle of nowhere. There was no sign of Justin or anybody else. She reached for her phone. But who could she call? Then she heard another car purring along and was ready to hitch, no matter the advice given by her mother. She breathed out thankfully as the car halted. On second thoughts it wouldn't be wise to ask for a lift from a stranger. She began to feel threatened and was cross she'd just been dropped off with no explanation. At least she could ask for directions.

'Hi,' she began, 'I wonder if you could . . . ' She stopped, her mouth dry, as Justin uncoiled himself from the driver's seat and stood in front of her.

'What do you wonder?' he asked, his head cocked to one side, a slight, teasing grin on his face.

Thea considered storming off, but then she really would be on her own in the middle of nowhere, which was a scary thought.

'Hey, I know you. No, don't tell me. I never forget a pretty face.' Justin grinned as he looked her over. 'You got run over by a boy on a bike, right? And you really are Thea Stafford from FPC? The production company?'

Thea nodded.

'Okay, I believe you. I've been caught out before by people trying to get close to me under false pretences.' He glanced at her case. 'Are you staying over?' he enquired giving it a small kick with his Kurt Geiger loafers.

Thea was at rock bottom now. She'd been humiliated enough. 'That's my business,' she retorted. 'I may be going on.'

'On where?' he persisted, his grin widening and a dimple visible through his stubble.

'I just wasn't sure what would be expected in the way of dress code,' she said, truthfully, all of a sudden deflated. She wished she was better at dealing with these sorts of situations. She was sure that Hermione would know exactly what to say and do, but would she really want to be like her?

As if aware of her unease, Justin laid a hand on her arm and squeezed it lightly. 'It's okay. I'm sorry, I wanted to pick you up, but I got delayed.'

Thea made a show of looking at her watch. 'Better get going or we won't have much time for the interview. Unless we do it here, is that what you're thinking?'

The twinkle in his eyes made her cringe as she realised the unintentional double entendre. Swiftly, she wheeled her bag over, put it into the boot and slipped into the passenger seat.

As he pulled away, she asked, 'How

far is it to your house?'

'The house? That shouldn't take too long, we're in the grounds of it already.'

'This belongs to you? All this woodland?' She watched wide-eyed as he nodded. She gulped, wondering if the questions she'd drafted for the interview were now pertinent. Never mind, she could wing it. But she liked to be organised. In her head, she drafted a new line-up of enquiries. With Justin likely to be a real distraction, she desperately hoped she'd remember it.

Thea was determined she wouldn't appear too impressed with Justin's house, but when they turned into the sweeping drive and the house eventually came into view, she couldn't help her unconcealed, mouth-open surprise. 'This is amazing. What a beautiful house. Oh, this is so great. I can't believe you live here. Wow.' Okay, so she couldn't do blasé without a rehearsal.

Justin chuckled. 'It's nice, yes.'

He parked the car, retrieved her bag and walked it and her up the steps to the front door. Then he gave a sheepish shrug and rang the bell. 'Forgot my key,' he admitted.

The wooden door creaked open like a Hammer Horror movie and Thea expected a wizened old crone to cackle and beckon them in with a bony finger. Instead a young woman with extremely short red hair said, 'Forgot your keys, didn't you?' She pushed between Justin and Thea, tossing a 'hi' in Thea's direction before disappearing around the back of the house.

Thea could have kicked herself. Just because she hadn't read lately of a romantic involvement in Justin's life, didn't mean there wasn't one. That young woman was his type; she had a self-assured air that Thea couldn't compete with. She may as well go home now. Then she reminded herself why she was here. It wasn't to get into Justin's heart or bed, it was to do an interview for the company where she was a dogsbody and wanted to claw her way up the ladder.

Justin led the way into the baronial hall and stood at the bottom of the impressive staircase. 'I have put a room at your disposal in case you want to rest, write or freshen up,' he said. 'I'll show you where it is, shall I?'

Thea followed him up the stairs, her eyes darting in all directions, wanting to take in all the unexpected things around her: the stained glass windows, a little console table with fresh flowers, pretty still life paintings and romantic landscapes. So absorbed was she in her surroundings, that when Justin stopped outside a door on the first landing, she didn't. They both looked down at Justin's expensive shoes and saw Thea's dusty trainer imprint on one of them. She'd have to shape up a bit or she'd be thrown out, and then what would she say to Dave?

Behind closed doors, out of sight of Justin, Thea did as good a repair job as she could to her make-up, and brushed her hair. Today was turning out to be a bit scary. She desperately wanted the interview to be a success, and she was surprised at her reaction to Justin. Of course, everyone wanted a piece of him; he was the hottest star of the moment. But Thea knew, felt, there was more to him than just movies. His whole face had lit with his megawatt smile after her accident, and she'd glimpsed hidden qualities beneath the façade.

Knowing that the time was marching along, Thea opened her notebook, which she preferred to a laptop much to Hermione's open disgust, and made notes about the day so far. They would jog her memory later. That done, she pulled out a pair of comfortable but stylish shoes from her bag and put them on. Then she opened the door and hoped she could find her way back to Justin through this vast mansion without a map.

'Hi,' he called as her feet hit the bottom stair.

'Hi,' she replied, wondering where his voice was coming from. In the large hall there was an echo, and it wasn't easy.

Justin appeared behind her brandishing what looked like a very sharp knife. 'I'm in the kitchen,' he said.

She trotted after him into the kitchen. 'This is a very big kitchen,' she said. She glanced at the huge wooden table in the middle of the room, which was covered in a vast variety of vegetables. She stopped herself from enthusing about it as she'd made enough of a fool of herself when she'd seen the house. She must try to be level-headed.

'I'm making lunch,' said Justin, using his sharp knife quickly and efficiently. 'Just soup and bread. Well, I'm making the soup, the breadmaker's made the bread.'

Thea's tummy growled at the mention of food. 'Can I help?' Thousands of women would love to be in her position, offering to help Justin Anderson cook.

'Sure. You can get out some plates and some cutlery. You'll have to root around for them. Rae chucks them in whichever cupboard or drawer takes her fancy.'

'That's your girlfriend, right?' Thea said, hoping to sound casual.

Justin stopped chopping long enough to throw her a blank look. 'Who? Rae? She's my sister. You just saw her, passed her at the front door.'

Thea felt elated, but kept her attention on discovering plates and spoons in the most unlikely places. She inhaled the delicious smell of vegetables and spices wafting through the room.

While Justin blitzed the soup, Thea cut the olive bread into thick chunks and got the butter out of the fridge. It was solid of course, so she just put the dish on the table.

She couldn't believe she was sitting in Justin Anderson's kitchen, having bread and soup. She scooped up another spoonful of spicy root vegetable soup. It was amazing just to be sitting next to him.

When they'd finished, the bowls looked clean enough to put away without being washed.

'You were as hungry as me, then?' said Thea.

'Sure. I was up about five this morning. I had to get to an early meeting.' He pushed the bowls to one end of the table. 'There's enough left for Rae if she comes back. She's vegetarian and our food is geared around that. Hope that's all right with you. She doesn't like to eat anything with a face.' Justin put his hand on her arm and she shivered involuntarily. 'Are you okay? Not coming down with something, I hope.'

Not unless it's Justin Anderson fever, thought Thea. She said, 'I'm fine. I'll be better now with food inside me. I'm sorry to take up your precious time. You seem so busy.'

'You're not putting me out. I agreed to the interview and I don't usually break my promises.'

Thea stood up and ran hot water into the sink before starting on the dishes.

'There's a dishwasher over there,'

Justin indicated.

'Nearly finished now,' remarked Thea. She was aware of him moving about behind her. Then he was picking up the dishes from the draining board and wiping them dry. 'I'd put them away, but Rae might not be able to find them,' said Thea, looking round the kitchen and noticing some large stainless steel bowls filled with what looked like a muesli of some sort on a shelf near the back door. As her head swivelled back towards Justin, their eyes met and he chuckled. Taking advantage of his good humour, Thea asked, 'Are they for us, too?' She pointed at the stainless steel dishes and giggled.

Justin's eyes sparkled, 'In a way, yes.'

Abruptly, he picked up a bowl, handed it to her, took one himself and said, 'Follow me.'

He yanked open the kitchen door. Once again, Thea had to hurry to keep up with Justin's long strides, wondering where they were going. He looked round and slowed his pace. They continued down a walkway between lawns and fruit trees. Then they came to a sectioned-off piece of land and Justin opened a gate and walked through without so much as a second glance in her direction. Looking at the mucky field, Thea was furious that her good shoes would get muddy. Why hadn't he told her they were going walking and given her time to change? However, she wouldn't let him see that she was put out. Slipping, she almost let the contents of her container spill onto the grass, but Justin was there, rescuing the bowl, but not Thea. She muttered to herself indignantly.

'Easy does it.' A strong arm came around her waist and helped her belatedly. The contact sent electricity through her.

'Thanks,' she said.

He glanced at her, but didn't say anything until they'd crossed the field and were entering another one by a five-bar gate which Justin held open for her.

As Thea went into the open area, she looked around and giggled, all thoughts of her dirty shoes gone from her mind. 'Your pets? How lovely. So this is their food?'

Then she took a closer look. The poor horses and donkeys had bones almost sticking through their skin. They looked tired and defeated. Horrified, she turned on her heel and strode towards the house determined to pack her things, call the animal cruelty people and get out of there as soon as she could. If this was the real Justin Anderson she wanted nothing to do with him.

She could hear Justin calling after her, but ignored him and started jogging to the house. How could she have misjudged the man? He'd seemed so caring. Should she phone the animal rescue people and then call a taxi or get away first and then call them? Justin caught up with her, grabbing her elbow.

'Hey, hold on, what's the matter? One minute you're doting on our donkeys and the next you're marching out on me.'

She turned to face him. 'I can't bear unkindness to animals,' she spat.

'Neither can I,' he said quietly.

'I've seen those creatures back there. How can you dare to say that?' She was angry with him and angry with herself for being so wrong about him.

'Because it's true. They aren't specifically mine. We, that is me and Rae, look after them. They've been abandoned by their owners. I won't go into the sordid details, but let's just say that there are some wicked, brutal people about. We give the animals a good home, there's nothing wrong with that, is there?'

Thea stood, trying to take in what Justin was saying. It was awful that people could be so nasty. How could anyone let animals starve?

'Come back with me. They're beginning to trust Rae and me and like being fussed over. Come on, Thea, meet them properly.'

Not knowing quite what to believe Thea's investigative streak came to the fore. Back at the field she looked at the pathetic donkeys and horses, inspecting their thin coats and emaciated bodies. Tears came into her eyes and she turned her head away. When she felt Justin's body against her, she curled into it and let herself be comforted.

Gradually her sobs subsided and she pulled away from him gently. 'Have you given them the food?' she asked, her voice cracking slightly.

'They've helped themselves.' Justin pointed at the empty bowls on the ground. 'Come on, I'll show you where we usually feed them.'

Thea's emotions were all over the place. Not only was she upset that these animals had been so ill-treated, she also wondered how she would ever find the real Justin Anderson. She felt this was only the tip of the iceberg.

The wooden shelter was really quite

cosy. The horses seemed fond of Justin, nuzzling him as he made a fuss of them. He showed her where they usually put the food and then picked up a broom from a corner to sweep out the soiled straw before preparing to put down clean.

'Can I help?' asked Thea, feeling useless.

'Sure. Can you muck out the donkey shelter?' He nodded across the field.

Thea picked her way over to the three-sided enclosure and started mucking that out. The donkeys were curious and came to see her. 'Hi, guys,' she greeted them. 'Come to make sure I'm doing it properly, eh?' She smiled as she worked, enjoying the practical task. Then, just as she moved to put down clean straw for them, she felt herself being pushed up against the side. 'What . . . ' One of the donkeys had her trapped and was attempting to bite her. 'Hey, stop that,' she said sternly and raised her arm to try and push it away. With that it reared up and kicked its back legs. Thea slipped and fell to the ground, getting covered in straw. She feared she would be trampled or badly kicked.

'Now, Milly, now then girl.' Relief flooded through Thea as Justin calmly talked to the donkey, took its harness and led it out into the field. He was soon back and helping Thea to her feet. She wasn't hurt, just shaken. Justin brushed straw off her clothes. 'Don't blame Milly, will you? It's going to be some time before she can trust humans again and meantime we have to forgive her little tantrums. You are all right aren't you?'

'I'm fine, but I'm not so sure about my shoes. One of my heels has broken off.' Thea looked down at her ruined shoes. In spite of the fright she'd just had, she unexpectedly felt very happy to be just where she was and she chuckled, pleased to hear not only Justin joining in, but also one of the donkeys braying.

* * *

'Would you like to stay for a few days?'

Thea choked on the wine she was sipping, wiped her mouth and said, 'Yes, I would.' She didn't know why she'd agreed so readily. It was madness accepting the invitation when she hardly knew Justin. What was wrong with her?

'I usually guard my privacy. And as long as you don't intrude too much . . .' he said, a smile taking the sting out of the words. Then his face once again broke into the full beam that Thea was growing to adore.

She watched Justin move around the large room, adjusting pictures, re-arranging cushions and smelling the fresh flowers in a pretty vase. He seemed nervous. Then he said, abruptly, 'I can't believe I'm asking you this, but we're a bit desperate at the moment with the daft hours I'm working and Rae's commitments. Would you be willing to lend a hand while you're here?'

Though she was surprised, she nodded and said, 'I'd love to. Around the house, do you mean? Or outside as well?'

'Both?' Justin's neat eyebrows rose. As Thea hesitated, he moved away. 'It doesn't matter, just a thought. I expect you want to get on with the interview.'

'I'd rather help,' she admitted, shyly. 'Although the interview is what I'm here for primarily. I was dithering because I haven't got the right sort of clothes.'

Justin laughed. 'I thought you were too good to be true. You women seem to put fashion before practicality.'

'That's just not true,' Thea protested. 'At least, not for me. I can't very well feed the horses in the sort of dress I brought in case we went to The Ritz for lunch. I can't see myself reaching the top cupboards in the kitchen or digging the potatoes up in my little black cocktail number.' She opened her mouth to say that she didn't have enough changes of underwear either, but felt herself reddening and closed it again.

Justin looked thoughtful. At last he came up with, 'Fair enough. In the wardrobe in your room there are a few pairs of jeans, and a couple of t-shirts and jumpers that you're welcome to use. Also thick socks. There are several pairs of boots near the back door, I'm sure there'll be some which fit you. Does that make your decision any easier?'

It did, but she couldn't help wondering who the clothes belonged to: an ex-girlfriend or even a current girlfriend. There had been plenty of pictures in magazines of Justin accompanied by gorgeous women attending glitzy functions. She put the thought from her mind. 'Perfect. I'd like to help out in any way I can. But what about Rae? Will she object to me being here?'

'Why would she object? Speaking of Rae, she should have been back for lunch. I expect she's on a mission to save animals somewhere. We'd better get into the kitchen and see what we can make for supper.'

* ★ ★

Thea found she was growing nervous as Rae's arrival neared. She peeled vegetables and made a salad. She eventually located some olive oil for the dressing. Then the back door thumped open and Rae came into the kitchen. 'Hi there.' She extended a grubby hand towards Thea, thought better of it and withdrew it. 'I'm Rae. Are you staying for supper?'

Thea started to awkwardly explain about helping out.

Justin butted in, 'I've asked Thea to stay for a few days. She's doing a profile on me for FPC, a production company.' Rae snorted. 'And you're pretty busy at the moment, so I thought an extra pair of hands would be useful.'

Rae ran her fingers through her short crop of hair. 'Those Bakers,' she burst out at Justin, 'how can they treat those poor pigs like that?'

Justin put a hand on her shoulder and squeezed it. 'You know what they're like. It's not the first time they've ill-treated their animals.'

'I'll make sure it's the last, though,' sniffed Rae.

Thea was intrigued, not only by the conversation, but also by the closeness of the two siblings.

Justin said, 'Go and clean up, Rae. You must be starving. We've enough here to feed us for the week.'

'No, I can't eat. I've got to get the pigs housed somewhere. They can't go in with the donkeys, they'll fight like cat and dog.' Then she clutched at Justin and howled with laughter, tears running down her face. 'Sorry, Justin, can't help it,' she gulped. 'You know what I'm like. I find all this so emotional I need to release the tension.'

Justin turned to Thea. 'The time to worry about Rae is when she doesn't laugh. But you'd better explain, Rae. You haven't done what I think you've done, have you?'

Rae nodded. 'Yep, I've brought them home. Honestly, Justin, they don't deserve to be treated like that.'

'I agree, but I'm afraid we may be in a lot of trouble. The Bakers might call the police. You've actually stolen their pigs.'

Rae was defiant. 'I don't care. I'm going to make them comfortable now.'

'If you'll wait for me to change, I can help,' volunteered Thea, almost looking forward to it. 'What sort of accommodation would they like? I imagine they're being booked in under full board?'

'I like you,' said Rae. 'Okay, let's leave Gordon Ramsay to the kitchen while we get on with the important jobs.'

★ ★ ★

Thea wasn't sure how she felt when they finally sat down to their meal that evening. She'd loved the pigs, although she was unsure how to handle them. Rae, on the other hand, had pushed and shoved them into place, found just the right spot and more or less out of nothing had constructed houses for them. The April evening had grown chilly, but she'd been nice and cosy in the borrowed jeans, t-shirt and jumper she'd helped herself to from the cupboard. When she and Rae returned to the house, they were both exhilarated from the physical exertion. Thea ran upstairs in her socked feet, showered and changed into her little black dress.

'Wow,' exclaimed Rae, 'you're showing me up now.'

'I haven't got much else.' Thea studied Rae. 'You look fine to me. I love your hair.' To Thea's surprise, Rae blushed and put her hand self-consciously to her head.

'Let's eat,' said Justin. They sat around the big kitchen table with Justin dishing out helpings of mixed-bean casserole with a cobbler topping, mashed swede, cabbage, and the salad Thea had prepared.

'So, Rae, how did you know about the pigs?' Justin asked.

'Veronica, she's the post woman,' Rae explained for Thea's benefit, 'told me that the animal-rescue people had been a few weeks ago, but in spite of everything they'd told the Bakers, the pigs were still being ill-treated. I wasn't prepared for them to suffer any longer. So I just took them.'

'As I said, you might be in a lot of trouble, but I'm behind you one hundred percent,' said Justin.

'And now we've got Thea and her company behind us as well.' Rae looked at Thea for confirmation.

Thea almost choked, nodded and then wondered what Dave and Hermione would think about the situation. There was silence except for the clanking of the cutlery. Justin frowned, but didn't say anything. When the plates had been cleared he said, 'If anyone's still hungry, there's an apple pie in the fridge and some ice cream in the freezer.'

Thea blew out her cheeks. 'Nothing more for me, thanks.' She risked a look at Justin. He wasn't anything like she'd imagined. Even a few hours ago she'd considered herself an intruder, but now she felt almost part of the family. Justin and Rae enjoyed an easy-going relationship and they both appeared to accept her as if they'd known her for ages. Although Thea loved her job, if she were asked to stay on here and be the general cook, bottlewasher and farmhand, then she was sure she'd say yes. Why were they so accepting? She admitted to herself that she was still a bit in awe of Justin because of his fame. She also admitted to herself that she found him very attractive, not just in a shallow physical sense, but on a deeper level.

'I can make tea,' Thea offered, 'or coffee.' She looked around the table. Having raided the freezer, Rae now sat with a large pot of cookie-dough ice cream, spooning it into her mouth.

'Rae always overcompensates when she's upset,' explained Justin quietly.

Rae seemed off in a world of her

own. Thea thought she must feel very strongly about the abuse which was going on. But then so must Justin. He took the animals in and looked after them as well. Thea sat thinking she should clear the table and load the dishwasher. Suddenly the back door opened with a bang. Two unkempt men filled the doorframe, one of them was wielding an iron bar. Justin leapt up and stood protectively between them and the two young women.

'Call the police, Rae,' he said over his shoulder.

'Stop just where you are.' The larger of the two men barged past Justin and swiped the phone from Rae's hand. It clattered to the floor. He took hold of the kitchen table with both hands, lifted it and let the dirty crockery and cutlery smash to the floor, then he banged the table down. 'I'm warning you, missy,' he spat at Rae, pushing his face right up close to hers. 'I want those pigs brought back first thing tomorrow morning.' Turning to his brother, he laughed viciously. 'Okay, Zach, do your stuff.'

Thea stared in terror as Zach brandished the iron bar. He swept everything from the work surfaces, smashed the pictures on the wall and the glass-fronted cupboards, then he walked over to Justin. 'Want your pretty face smashing too? He'd have to be a villain in the pictures then, wouldn't he, Unwin?'

'Just shut up and get on with it, Zach.'

Zach swung the iron bar back. Thea gasped in horror.

'No, you idiot, don't hit him now. That's for later. Finish off the kitchen.' Unwin watched as Zach continued his destruction.

'Right, let's get out of here,' Unwin finally said with a ghastly leer. 'You call the cops and you can watch the animals die slowly, one by one. A horrible death.' Then the brothers lumbered out of the door.

4

They studied the mess around them. Then Justin took the women into the sitting room and poured them each a glass of wine. 'I think this might steady us. Not sure brandy's a good idea.'

'At least we hadn't cleaned up the kitchen,' said Rae.

'We should call the police.' Thea was indignant about the attack and also very frightened. She tried to hide her fear as Rae was putting up such a brave front. The more Thea found out about Rae, the more she admired her. Her gruff exterior hid her gentle nature. It was obvious that she and her brother were supportive and loyal to each other as well as happy living together. Looking at Rae, Thea wondered what was going through her mind. It was scary enough to have witnessed the horrible incident, but for that hate to be directed at you personally must be chilling. Yet to look at Rae, you'd think she was used to such events and simply took them in her stride.

'No,' replied Justin very quietly. 'We won't be calling the police. I know I told Rae to call them, but that was a bluff, I had a feeling we wouldn't be allowed to get that far. I mean it, Thea. You must promise that you won't even think of it. There's too much at stake.'

'All right,' sighed Thea, understanding that he didn't want his sister arrested for stealing the pigs. There was also the threat to the animals which the intruders had made. She drained her glass and stood up. 'At least let me help you get things straight in the kitchen.'

'You must go to bed.' He took hold of her shoulders and gave her an encouraging push towards the door.

'I'm out of here, I need to talk to Veronica,' said Rae, pushing past Thea.

★ ★ ★

63

It took Thea a while to remember where she was. It was the absolute quietness which confused her. She couldn't possibly be at her home in London. Then it dawned on her that she was not only staying overnight at Justin Anderson's house, but she was also helping with the house and animals. How weird was that? While the responsibilities seeped into her waking brain, she dragged herself to the bathroom for a hot shower, rummaging in the cupboard for clean jeans, t-shirt and an all-too-welcome jumper. Although it was April, there were cold days. As she pulled the big jumper over her head and smoothed it down over her slim hips, there was a tap at the door. She yanked it open and saw Rae.

'I brought tea,' Rae said, handing over a large mug of steaming liquid.

Thea grabbed it gratefully, and sipped. 'Absolutely what I need,' she smiled. 'Thank you. And I'm sorry if I overslept, but I'm not that used to heavy physical work. I didn't think I'd get a wink after the drama of those awful men trashing everything. I don't think I reacted well at all. I froze.'

'You were great. It was scary, wasn't it? Anyway, I came to say thank you for all the help you gave us. Justin reminds me occasionally that my manners are not what they should be.' Rae made to go back along the landing.

'Rae, may I ask you something?' Thea said. Receiving a nod, she plunged on. 'What is it you do? Do you have a job outside the house? I'm being nosy, but you always seem to be hurrying off somewhere.'

'I belong to several groups,' she explained. 'Mostly to do with animal protection. Like I said, Veronica can often spot a stray dog or a lost cat. I try to help with getting them back to their owners. And then there's the other extreme like the Bakers who seem to derive pleasure from making people and animals suffer. I suppose I should get a proper job, eh?'

'No, not at all. I think you're

fantastic, doing all those things, Rae. You *are* doing a proper job in my opinion.' Thea yawned and looked at her watch. 'Is Justin up?' she asked. 'I haven't even thought about getting breakfast for everyone. At home I only have toast.' Her voice trailed away.

'No sweat. He's at the studio. Won't be back until mid-morning. I've put some porridge on. I usually do it the old-fashioned way.' Rae said in an outrageous Scottish accent, making Thea laugh.

'But the kitchen . . . However did you manage?'

'Justin fixed things as best he could,' shrugged Rae. 'There's a maintenance company coming in later to put things back into working order. In the meantime we'll just have to work around the mess. I've got to go and see to the horses now.'

Thea hesitated. 'I seem to be togged up for that sort of thing today. Can I help you?'

'Okay,' said Rae. 'It'll be more fun

with someone else along.'

'Let me see what's in the house for lunch and supper and I'll join you. I think I can remember my way to Milly and her friends.'

Thea gingerly pushed the kitchen door open, experiencing a flashback to the previous night's violence. Everything was fairly neat and tidy and there was a workable space on the table. Rae's pan of porridge was simmering on a rather dusty stove which, thankfully, was still functioning. Thea knew she'd just have to get on with things and not make a fuss. She gave the porridge a stir and turned off the heat.

Thea searched the cupboards, fridge and freezer, deciding on food for the day. She flicked on the radio. The voice she heard certainly hit all the right buttons with her. She stood still in the middle of the kitchen, with butterflies in her stomach. Then the presenter said, 'You'll all recognise the voice of Justin Anderson. That was an excerpt from his latest film . . . '

Thea didn't hear the rest, she was too busy trying to calm down. She told herself that her reaction was just because it was unexpected, it had nothing to do with it being Justin. She fancied him when she watched his films, that was true, just like Hermione had reminded her. What was it she had said? A here today, gone tomorrow sort. Thea would like to get to know him, but why would he be interested in her with all the beautiful people around him? She had to be sensible. She'd do her interview, help Rae with the feeding and mucking out, try not to poison anyone with her cooking and then get back home.

After hanging her washing on the line, she made her way to the fields to find Rae. She heard her before she saw her. 'Milly, you do that one more time and it'll be donkey burger for you, miss.'

'Hi, Rae. Having trouble?' giggled Thea as she held out a none too trusting hand to Milly.

'You'd think she'd like a carrot of her own, wouldn't you? But no she has to have the one I've just given Harry. That's the bay over there, the one without a carrot.'

'Should I have made up the horses' feed? I've no idea how, but I don't mind having a go.'

'It's fine. It's quite a complicated recipe of a sloppy bran mash mixed with molasses and a few other ingredients. That's why we make it up in the kitchen. If you'd finish the mucking out and get some clean water from the tap for them, I can go back and do that. I've done the pigs.'

'They're sweeties, aren't they?' commented Thea, smiling. She didn't want to bring up the subject of their awful owners in case she upset Rae, who seemed in a good mood now.

'They're gorgeous. I can't imagine why anyone would want to eat them,' scowled Rae.

'What was that you were saying about donkey burgers?'

'Can't hear you,' grinned Rae, before running out of the field.

Thea picked up the rake and started on her chores. She'd never envisaged herself as a farmhand before. She talked to the animals as she hefted straw and water, giving them a pat when they came near. Thea had never had pets and she was surprised how much she enjoyed being with these poor, neglected creatures. Pausing in her work, she lifted her face to the sky and breathed in deeply. It was wonderful here, everything from the countryside to the company. She looked at the view across the valley to the wooded hills beyond. Standing still for a moment, she listened. The only sounds were the animals snuffling and the birds singing. There was something special about being in this environment which she couldn't put her finger on.

'Not sure who's enjoying that the most, you or them.'

Thea jumped and spilled water over Milly's foot. 'Now look what you made me do.' It was Justin. 'I'll get you something to eat when I've finished this,' she called. 'Unless you ate at the studio.'

Justin caught hold of her arms to stop her activity. 'You don't have to run the place single-handedly,' he whispered, his warm breath soft on Thea's ear.

Pulling herself free, she said, 'You asked me to help in the house and out here. I just want to do a good job for you, for you and Rae.'

Justin let go of her and put out his hand to Milly who, traitor that she was, nuzzled into his tummy and let herself be stroked and talked to. 'Good girl, Milly. Let's go over here, shall we, away from the nasty woman with the pail of water. She made your feet wet, she put her footprints on my best shoes, we'll be better off out of her way.'

Thea finished her work, put away her tools and went back towards the house. Hauling off her boots at the back door, she brushed herself down before having a thorough wash at the sink. Then she noticed a box of vegetables on the kitchen table. How had they got there? Surely Justin hadn't picked them up on his way home.

'Hi there, ma'am,' came a familiar voice.

'Toby?' squealed Thea. 'Nice to see you. No strange young women to pick up today, then?'

'No, ma'am,' he smiled. 'Just the veg.' He gestured towards the box with his big hand.

'I'd better warn you that I'm cooking, if you're planning on staying for lunch,' said Thea.

'No I'm not, thanks,' replied Toby, heading for the door.

'Hey,' called Thea, 'I was only kidding. Well, I am cooking, but it won't be too bad, I'm sure.'

'I'm on Justin's time and I don't usually eat with the family.' Toby turned and smiled. 'I eat meat.'

★ ★ ★

'This lentil pâté's great,' mumbled Rae, her mouth full.

Thea smiled, pleased with the compliment. Rae had insisted that they start, declaring herself famished. Thea had no idea where she put all the food, as she was stick thin. When Justin came in, he selected a can of coconut water from the fridge and sat down next to Rae. 'Good morning?'

'Fair,' said Rae. 'Those horses are looking a bit fatter and their coats are getting shinier.'

'And what do you think of the pigs?'

'They're gorgeous. I'm going out to see them again in a minute.' Rae stuffed more bread laden with pâté into her mouth.

The phone rang and Rae rushed off to answer it. She came back a different woman, looking sad and distraught. Justin was on his feet and by her side. 'What's up?'

'The Bakers. They've got some sort of injunction against me for taking their pigs. I've got to give them back.'

'That's outrageous,' fumed Justin. 'They can't have them. Especially after their performance yesterday.'

Thea admired their spirit and already hated the Bakers as vehemently as Justin and Rae did. 'Can I help?' she offered, but she wasn't heard as Rae ran from the room shouting that she'd see them hang.

Justin sat down and resumed his meal with an equanimity quite at odds with his earlier anger. 'Rae gets very upset when faced with cruelty of any kind. She experienced something very upsetting when she was very young. It shaped her life,' he explained.

'What happened to make her feel so strongly?'

'Rae always loved animals, but when she was about ten and playing in the street on her bike, there was a commotion in one of the front gardens. She could hear squealing, but also laughter and cheering. There was a group of children torturing a stray cat. It was so frightened and badly hurt it couldn't escape. Absolutely livid, she shouted at the children and scared them so much they all ran off.'

'That sounds like just the sort of thing Rae would do. She must have been terribly upset.'

'Yes, she was. My parents had an awful time with her. She wanted to find the children and show them what they'd done and try to get them to realise that their conduct was unacceptable.'

'What about the cat? Did it survive?'

'Yes, the vet gave it painkillers and stitched up the worst of the wounds. Then, of course, Rae nursed her back to health, but she was always very timid and scared of new people. Poor Tiddles, that's what Rae named her, just couldn't trust anyone again.'

'She was lucky Rae rescued her.'

'She was lucky to have Rae to care for her as well. From that moment Rae vowed to help as many animals as she could. She was forever bringing home underweight hedgehogs, injured birds, even a fox that had been hit by a car. She lost interest in school and left as soon as she was old enough. Caring for animals is her passion.'

'I admire her.'

'I definitely wouldn't like to be the Bakers when she meets up with them again.' He looked at Thea and grinned thinly.

'Don't you think one of us should have gone with her?' asked Thea, her mind racing from road accidents to murder.

'She'll be fine. I have a feeling she'll drive halfway to their farm, pull in somewhere and think it through calmly. Then she'll come back and it'll be as if nothing's happened. But I'm sure she'll give the Bakers a piece of her mind when she does see them, even if it's in court.'

'But she'll have to return the pigs?' Thea couldn't bear to think of them being returned to such a place with those awful people.

'I can't see Rae agreeing to that

unless someone from the authorities comes here and physically carries them away.' Justin shrugged as he helped himself to more food. 'So this interview. Are you still doing it?' He looked at Thea. 'That jumper of mine suits you.'

Thea pulled at the soft wool. She'd no idea it was Justin's jumper. She'd assumed it belonged to one of his ex-girlfriends. 'I'm sorry,' she said, about to yank it off. 'It was in the cupboard, you said to help myself.'

Once again that full beam smile radiated towards her. 'I was only teasing. Of course you can wear it. Take it home with you if you like.'

Thea was enjoying living with Justin and Rae. Even though she'd only been there for a very short time, she already felt a close bond with them. But she had her job to go back to unless Hermione had engineered things to get rid of her. Although Dave had been firm in his promise that he would keep her on.

Trying to put the animals, the Bakers

and Rae out of her mind, Thea said, 'Yes, I do want the interview, please. Let me just clear the table and I'll get my notes and questions.'

Justin stood up, taking her hand. '*I'll* clear the table. You get what you need. I'll put the coffee on.'

When Thea returned to the kitchen, she was surprised to see it tidy with no sign of the recent meal evident. She also noticed the stainless steel bowls containing the mixture for the animals. Was it only yesterday that she'd arrived at this mansion owned by a film star? So much had happened, it was difficult to take in. However, she knew she must remain focused on the interview as that was her primary reason for being here; her *only* reason, she admonished herself. *And don't forget that, Thea.* She brought her hand to her mouth. Had she said that out loud? Justin would be thinking he'd been landed with a madwoman. Sneaking a glance at him, she didn't think he'd heard. She flopped down at the table and took the mug of coffee which Justin handed to her. She made sure he was comfortable with the interview being recorded as well as her taking written notes, and began her questions.

'How old were you when you decided to be an actor?' Thea began, shifting in her seat, hoping Justin would appreciate the questions she'd come up with.

'I've been an actor since the age of six,' he grinned. 'I was a tree in a school production of 'In the Forest.''

'And you moved on to speaking parts from there?' Thea kept her head down, her lips quivering slightly.

Justin nodded. 'At secondary school I was the white rabbit in 'Alice's Adventures in Wonderland'. I'm late, I'm late, for a very important date,' he recited.

'Very good,' encouraged Thea, although it wasn't rocket science to remember *those* lines. 'And what did your family think?'

'Rae said I was rubbish, but I didn't care what she thought, I thought I was brilliant.' Justin waited, then said, 'Hey, you're not writing this down.'

'Do you really think your audience wants to hear that you thought you were wonderful?'

Justin nodded, 'Certainly, but if you like we can move on.'

Thea was annoyed he didn't seem to be taking any of it seriously. 'So when did Izaak Flanagan come on the scene?'

'About five years ago. It was a wonderful opportunity. It wasn't just a heart-throb, romantic casting. It was futuristic, escapist and a story of moral fortitude. Izaak sort of summed up everything I wanted to be.'

'Do you think you've lived up to him in your own life?'

'Interesting question. In a way it would be good to think so, but the circumstances he finds himself in are so far removed from how we live our lives today I'm afraid I can't answer the question.'

'Do you enjoy having women throw themselves at you?'

'Of course. It's part of the job. But I know better than to take them seriously.'

'Is there anyone special in your life? Has there ever been a scandal surrounding you?' Thea was cross with herself for lumping the two questions together. She should have waited for his response to the first one; the one she desperately wanted to know the answer to. Now she couldn't backtrack without making it obvious.

'No doubt there's been some gossip, but to the best of my knowledge I haven't been mixed up in anything nefarious. But what have your investigations into my life come up with?'

Thea looked up from her writing, but didn't answer his question. She didn't want to interrupt his flow. 'What would you have done with your life if you hadn't become an actor?' she asked.

'Probably worked on a market stall selling fruit and veg,' he answered unhesitatingly. 'I did that in the school holidays. The dad of a mate of mine had a stall and we used to get up at the crack of dawn and hump crates about in the market.'

'Then fame and fortune came knocking at your door?'

'Not that easily actually. I had to do the knocking and I soon realised that if I didn't make a real effort to follow my dream there were at least a hundred others waiting to walk over me to get to the star's dressing room.'

'And now what do your family think of you?' As Thea wrote, she found herself engrossed in Justin Anderson's story.

He fidgeted. 'I don't really want to answer personal questions like that,' he said.

'But you've been so open about everything else,' said Thea. She leant forward to assure Justin. 'I'm not going to pry. If you're not happy that's fine. We'll move on, shall we? Can you tell me a bit about your other passions? Hobbies, pastimes, guilty pleasures?'

'Looking after a menagerie, walking

in muddy fields, cooking, and lending attractive young women my jumpers.'

Thea's pen moved swiftly, taking down what he said. As she came to the last bit, she realised he was pulling her leg. But she wouldn't react. Without lifting her head, she added, 'And have you a favourite recipe you'd like to share with our viewers?'

'Touché,' he said.

Thea looked up. 'I think it's time to stop now.' She wanted to ask more probing questions, but didn't want to overdo it especially as he was being so helpful and cooperative. 'I'll have to have another session with you though and add some more depth. Is that all right?'

'Sure. It's fine. Tell me, why are people so interested in me?'

One look at him told Thea he didn't want to be reassured that he was God's gift to the Universe, he genuinely wanted to know.

'Apart from being a sex symbol, you've gained a vast following from the films. Men want to be Izaak Flanagan, women want men who *are* Izaak Flanagan. A larger than life person, someone who'll love and protect them as well.'

'But that's not Justin Anderson.'

'That's why I'm doing the interview,' said Thea, standing up and gathering her sheets of paper.

'Will you need our password for the Wi-Fi?' Justin grabbed some pages which had worked loose and were floating around the floor.

'Yes, please. I don't use a computer for interview notes as I prefer good old pen and paper. But Google would be handy.'

'If you need one, there's a computer in the room next to yours. Rae's got hers in her room.'

'It's okay, I've brought my laptop for emails and things. But as I just said my interview notes will be handwritten. I'll let you read them.'

Justin's eyes narrowed. 'How's your arm? I'd forgotten about it. It must be painful, especially after all the work you've had it doing.'

'It's okay. Now please excuse me, and thanks.'

'Here's the Wi-Fi password.' Justin handed her a card.

Thea padded up the stairs to the sanctuary of her room. Her head was thumping and she had an uneasy feeling in her insides. It couldn't be the close proximity to Justin as she'd given herself a good talking to over that and knew she'd be better off just to treat him as any interviewee. Also, the tenderness in her arm hadn't gone away, it was still very sore and she'd be glad to rest it. In the meantime, however, she had an interview to write up. Then she'd decide what to do next.

★   ★   ★

Discarding her dusty clothes and wrapping herself in a huge bathrobe, Thea sat at the table in her room and flicked through her notes. Pleased to have made such a good start, she pulled a block of paper towards her and started writing.

When a good few sheets were filled, she stretched out her hands and yawned. Scanning the pages, she thought it would be a good idea to ask Justin some more off-the-wall questions and for that, she needed the help of Google.

As soon as she switched on her laptop she knew she was going to have trouble as it took far longer than usual to start up. Then the cursor wouldn't move and after trying everything possible she finally gave in. Although Justin had invited her to use the computer, she felt awkward as she went into the room. Thankful that it was switched on, she sat down and typed in the words Justin Anderson. There were a few entries she'd seen before about his film career and some awards he'd won. Of course, Thea being a real fan had seen the films and knew about his prizes. She'd draw on her genuine admiration to make the profile spring to life for the viewer. However, she wasn't so arrogant as to be convinced she knew it all. There might well be something to learn from searching more. Thea skimmed over most of the articles as she wanted to know the real Justin, not the headline-grabbing one. About to try another search, her attention was taken by a newspaper picture of a younger Justin, as a boy almost, and two young girls. The caption underneath said: Justin Anderson, together with his younger sister and the girl his parents adopted. It was an admirable gesture as the girl was in such poor health.

Thea stared at the screen, her eyes glittering. Could it be Rae? She'd seemed fine and had such energy and vitality. Looking intently at the picture, she became surer than ever that the article was about Rae.

'I might have guessed you'd find that.' Justin had come into the room, without Thea noticing. He stood by the computer, his back to her, looking out of the window. 'That's a headline grabber, isn't it?'

'Do they mean Rae?' whispered Thea.

'Rae?' Immediately Justin turned and looked at the screen. 'You think the article's about Rae?'

'I . . . I don't know. It's difficult to know who they're talking about . . . and the picture's a few years old, isn't it?' stammered Thea.

'Tell me what you make of it,' muttered Justin. He nodded towards the screen.

'I can see a picture of you and your two sisters,' replied Thea, conscious now of Justin's breath on her neck. 'One of them is Rae and the other is . . . well, I suppose she's your other sister.'

'Right so far,' acknowledged Justin. 'Anything else?'

Thea turned her head and found herself looking into his flinty eyes. 'One of your sisters is not well.'

'And?' persisted Justin.

'I wondered if it was Rae who wasn't well. She seemed to have a lot of energy with the horses and pigs. I like her and I'm sorry if she's got a health problem.'

Justin straightened up, a small smile now on his lips and his eyes softened. 'I think I believe you.'

Thea frowned as she tried to understand what he meant. 'Why wouldn't you believe me?'

'The media have been after us for a long while. I thought all the hounding was at last over. That woman, what's her name? Henrietta Claptrap?'

In spite of the seriousness of the conversation, Thea's laugh escaped like bubbles from an uncorked bottle of champagne. Instantly, she apologised. 'Hermione Clutterbuck,' she corrected him.

'Whatever. Anyway, *she* didn't mention my family and I thought that finally we were in the clear. Now you come along. You're a problem, Thea.

On the one hand, I like and trust you, but on the other, I've still got to be wary of the enemy.'

'But I'm not going to put out anything that you don't want me to. And I don't see why your sister's life has to be included in a profile on you.'

Justin was quiet for a long time. Then he said, 'I'd like to believe you. But it's a chance of a scoop, isn't it? Can I really trust you?'

'I'd like you to,' admitted Thea, feeling her cheeks grow rosy. 'If you can't, you can take the interview notes and tear them up. Now, if you'll excuse me, I'm going to get dressed so that I can get on with my other jobs around the house and grounds.'

Thea let herself out of the room, pulling the bathrobe tightly round her, leaving her written-up interview on the desk next to the computer. She'd hate him to tear it up, but she'd hate it more if Justin didn't trust her.

★ ★ ★

Downstairs in the kitchen again, preparing the evening meal, Thea couldn't get Justin and his sisters out of her mind. There was no way she'd reveal Justin's family secrets for a sensational story. On the one hand, she could understand Justin's concern, but she was hurt that he felt he wasn't sure about her.

Later she busied herself vacuuming the downstairs rooms. If Rae was poorly, she wouldn't want to be doing housework as well as going on rescue missions. And Justin had enough to do at the studio and then feeding the animals when he got back. It was strange they had no daily help. With thoughts of the Anderson household scurrying around her head, she didn't hear Justin until he came and stood in front of her, making her jump.

'I've been into your room,' he confessed. 'Only to drop off your interview pages. I left them on the floor just inside the door.'

'So you've decided to trust me?'

'I have,' smiled Justin. 'By the way, so that you needn't worry quite so much, let me tell you that Rae is not the sister with the illness. It's Grace who is the poorly one.'

Thea nodded her head as she took in this information. 'Whoever it is, I'm sorry.'

Justin's hand reached out to Thea, its warmth cutting through her sadness. 'Come with me when I visit her tomorrow?'

Thea was surprised. Justin had told her how protective he was of his sisters and now he was asking her to join them. He seemed determined to let her know he trusted her. There had never been any doubt in her mind. She would never knowingly let him down. She smiled at him, 'Thank you.' She felt a bond had been established between them. 'In the meantime, I'd better finish this. I expect Rae will be in a justifiable strop. She'll need a sympathetic ear.'

'It's okay, I'll deal with Rae. You can

do the mucking out of the horses, carry the feed down to the field and fill up the water troughs. Oh, and say hello to Milly.'

'Yes, of course I will,' said Thea, rather put out at the thought of missing the gossip. What a cheek the man had. He was really messing her about. One minute he appeared anxious to let her know he trusted her and wanted her company, and the next he was more or less telling her to stop being nosy. She had a good mind to refuse to see to the feed and water in the field, but she couldn't bring herself to be that mean.

Justin put his arms around her for a brief moment. Then he kissed her lightly on the cheek and said, 'I was only kidding. Of course you can listen to Rae's rant and then we'll all go down to the animals. That suit you?'

It suited Thea very well indeed, but the kiss and cuddle suited her even better.

★ ★ ★

93

Thea stayed in the kitchen. It had meant nothing to him, but she'd liked it when he'd held her close. Already the feel of his soft lips on her cheek and the wonderful clean smell of him were fading from her memory just a little. The good feeling inside her remained.

The kitchen was as tidy as anyone could make it given the circumstances, and a large saucepan of vegetarian chilli was simmering on the stove, sending an enticingly rich aroma around the room. Thea had found an old cookery book while she was rummaging for bay leaves and now she sat at the table and turned the pages.

Thea was engrossed in the Victorian recipes when Rae and Justin came in.

'They'll wish they'd never been born,' fumed Rae. 'Don't worry, Thea, I've only come back for a large, sharp knife or a cleaver of some sort.'

'Settle down, Rae,' instructed Justin. 'You know you can't just go and do them in.'

'So I should simply sit down with a

cup of tea and have a chat about it, is that what you're saying?' Rae stomped around the kitchen, opening and banging shut drawers and cupboards.

Justin raised his eyebrows at Thea, a smile tweaking his lips, the dimple faintly denting his cheek.

Abruptly, Rae flung herself on a chair next to Thea. 'What've you got there?'

'Certainly not a cleaver,' replied Thea, who'd been a bit wary of Rae during her outburst.

Rae shrugged. 'I do get to the stage where my temper takes over, I'm afraid. He's always on at me about it.' She looked up at Justin. 'Sorry.'

'Is there anything you can do about the animals?' Justin's face took on a serious look. 'Poor things. Do they have to be returned?'

'Er, um,' Rae grabbed Thea's hand. 'I've involved you.'

'Rae, you shouldn't have done that,' barked Justin. 'Thea's here to interview me. She's already been put upon by us getting her to do housework and mucking out.'

Feeling things were getting out of control, Thea ventured, 'Involved in what way?'

Rae's eyes grew large and a conspiratorial grin broke across her face. 'I said we've got the TV people down and that they're doing an interview.'

Rae looked triumphant, but Justin looked as if he were about to explode. Before he could open his mouth, Thea said, 'It's the truth, I'll give you that.' She relaxed a little, assessing that Rae's tantrum had abated. However, she wasn't prepared for the bear hug that the skinny girl gave her. If she hadn't been sitting down, she'd have been knocked down by its force.

'What did the Bakers say to that?' enquired Justin, setting out mugs and searching hopefully in the biscuit tin.

Rae darted a look at Thea and Justin. 'As a matter of fact they were a bit scary. I marched into the yard and had my rant and then got out of there.' So

Justin had been wrong in his assumption of what Rae would do.

'You should be careful what you get yourself into, Rae,' murmured Justin. 'You know what they're capable of.'

'You're right, but I was so angry. All I could think of was the sweet pigs and how those awful men had neglected them. They backed down a bit. I'm sure the thought of Thea on their case scared them stiff.'

'What happens when they find out I'm not taking it any further?' Brother and sister looked at Thea. 'You expect me to do a piece on them?' she squeaked.

'Of course we do,' Rae replied. Justin just nodded.

Thea looked at them. Justin, a man who was known throughout the world, more or less, a man whom she was growing very fond of, and Rae, a passionate young woman driven by a cause. Thea knew it was a combination she would not be able to resist. Then she decided she didn't want to. She agreed with them. 'Leave it with me. I'll see what I can do, but we have to be careful. We don't want them to carry out their threat to hurt the animals.'

* * *

With tea and sympathy dispensed to Rae, the chores outside completed and supper eaten, Thea retired to her room.

If she was to follow through with her promise to help the Andersons with the Bakers, she would have to contact Dave. Not sure who would pick up his emails at the office and not wanting to give away Justin's private details, Thea decided that a phone call would be best. She'd have to leave it until the morning now, but she worked out what she wanted to say to him.

Snuggling under the duvet, her arm still aching a little, she thought about the next day. Tomorrow she would go with Justin to visit his other sister, Grace. The exciting thought of being with Justin didn't make for a good night's sleep. Even after all the physically taxing work she'd done that day, she still tossed and turned. At what she guessed was about two in the morning, she crept downstairs to make some hot milk. She'd look awful if she didn't get some sleep, and dark bags under her eyes would not make Justin think of her as anything other than his interviewer.

As she was about to push open the kitchen door, she heard voices, or rather one voice. Someone was talking on the phone. It was Justin. Wanting to know who he was talking to, but knowing she shouldn't be nosy, she turned round to go upstairs again. Nevertheless, she did catch the words: 'Of course I love you. See you soon.'

She scuttled up the stairs, the words turning her dream to a nightmare.

5

Thea awoke with butterflies in her tummy. Their cause was quite obvious. She had to ring Dave and then she had to spend a day with Justin. Now that she knew he had a woman he loved, there was no way he'd look at her. On the plus side though, it didn't matter a bit that she looked awful. Annoyed with herself for even thinking for a moment that this man would be interested in her gauche self, she stepped under the shower and turned it to cold, yelping at the force and iciness of it.

When she rang Dave, she was surprised at his eagerness to promote the poor creatures which the Andersons had taken under their wing. 'You should see them, Dave,' said Thea. 'Poor little things, shivering with fright when a stranger approaches them, thin to the point of emaciation. You can count their ribs.'

'Okay, Thea, don't go into the gruesome descriptions with me, leave that for the exposé.'

'Justin's sister is marvellous with them. She looks after them and never counts the cost to herself. I promise you won't regret it if you do the programme. I'll do my best to make it extra special.'

'Well done, Thea, another achievement for you, but I'll need to check up on the legal aspect and get back to you. How's the interview going? Are you managing to meet up somewhere locally? Don't forget you've got quite a generous entertainment allowance.'

'I'm staying at his house, Dave. Didn't I say?' Thea had no idea if she'd told him or not.

'What? Are you sure that's a good idea? What's the set up? Is it just the two of you? I'm not sure I like it, Thea.'

Thea grinned to herself. 'I'm perfectly safe, Dave. Rae, that's his sister, she lives here too, remember the one who does the animal rescue. It's fine, really. And don't worry about the expense account, we hardly spend any money.' A thought struck her. 'I could donate some of it to Rae for the animals' board and lodging if you like.'

Dave sent a bellow of laughter down the phone line. 'Just make sure you look after yourself and remember I'm just at the end of a telephone.'

'You're a sweetie,' said Thea, before remembering he was her boss and that it wasn't a very professional remark to make.

'Right then, I must go. Have a nice day,' said Dave.

Thea was determined that she *would* enjoy her day; she didn't need the approval of a man, even Justin Anderson, to fulfil her. She brushed off her strawberry-coloured trainers and pulled them on. Teamed with a fresh pair of jeans from the cupboard and her own top, she felt confident enough to face the outing. Peering in the mirror, she decided a little make-up would improve her appearance and applied some midnight-blue mascara, and a little gloss to her mouth. Smacking her lips together, she plucked her bag from the bed and went downstairs.

'Coffee?'

'Please, Rae,' smiled Thea. At least there was no sign of Justin. She sat at the table and sipped the strong coffee Rae put in front of her.

'Croissant?' A plate of freshly warmed pastries was waved under her nose. She took one and asked, 'What's this? Feed Thea day?'

Rae shrugged. 'It's good to start the day on a full stomach.'

Thea's eyes narrowed. 'So you've had something, too?'

Rae avoided her gaze and fidgeted with her cup. 'Shall we visit the animals after breakfast?'

'Well, I was expecting to go out with Justin. He said we're going to visit Grace. Will you come with us?'

Rae looked puzzled. 'But Justin's at the studio this morning. What time did he tell you he'd pick you up?'

'He didn't say. I'd forgotten about the studio. Never mind, I'll just get on with things here.' Inside she was disappointed. She *had* forgotten about the studio and Justin had said nothing to remind her. 'I hope he won't be too tired afterwards.' Thea thought back to the night-time conversation she'd overheard. Then Justin would have had to be up very early for the studio. While she couldn't stop herself from feeling sorry for him and admiring his devotion to his work, a part of her still pondered about the woman he'd said he loved. Okay, it was only a phone call and Thea didn't know all the facts. It still niggled, though. Maybe they met at the studio and that was why Justin bounded off there every morning. Thea recognised her jealousy and knew she'd just have to be patient and wait for Justin to get home and let her know the timetable for the day.

Rae paced around the kitchen. 'You have to understand that I do love

Grace. I've always thought of her as my proper sister rather than an adopted one.' She clamped a hand in front of her mouth. 'Oh no, have I let the cat out of the bag?'

Thea hurried to reassure her. 'It's all right, I already found out from googling. This article said one of Justin's sisters was adopted. It also said that one of the sisters had a health issue. At first I thought it was you.'

'Me? Heavens, no. I'm stinking fit.' She plonked herself down on a chair next to Thea. 'If I could, I'd give Grace half my strength.' Rae looked so unhappy, Thea put an arm around her shoulders.

'So, will you be visiting Grace with us, when Justin gets here?'

'I'll think about it. I never know what to say to her and usually end up talking about myself and all the things I've been rushing around doing and then I feel guilty when I come home that I've made her feel worse because she has so little energy.'

'Shall I pick some flowers or something to take to her?'

'What a lovely thought. What could we pick? Tulips, daffodils and those enormous white daisies. Would that do?'

'Sounds great. And do you think we could put some rosemary from the herb garden in with it. You know, rosemary for remembrance, so she knows you're thinking about her.'

Rae jumped up. 'Shall we do it now? I'll get secateurs. What shall we wrap them in?' She raced off like a child out to play, with Thea right behind her.

With a beautiful bunch of flowers and herbs ready to take, Rae's high spirits continued. 'Come on,' she said, grabbing Thea's hand. 'I'll show you Justin's toys. Did you know he collects cars?' Rae led the way to a large outbuilding tucked away at the back of the house. She unlocked the padlock, went inside and switched on the overhead lights.

'What do you think?'

'I had no idea he collected vehicles. All different types. I don't know anything about cars,' Thea confessed.

'Me neither. All I know is that one's green and that one's red.' The two young women laughed.

Thea realised the red car was the one Justin had picked her up in when Toby had dropped her at the gate of his estate. A lot had happened since then. She walked over to the green sports car.

Rae followed her. 'That's racing green. Have you seen the number plate? Cool, isn't it?'

Thea saw, JUST IN. 'It says Porsche Cayman on the back.' Then she wandered round the barn looking at the other vehicles. 'Will Justin mind that you've shown me these?'

'No, why should he, it's not some sort of secret, is it?'

'I didn't find anything about this hobby when I googled him.'

'It'll be good for your thing about Justin, won't it?'

'It will. Thank you, Rae. We could

shoot in here and maybe get him to drive one or two of the cars, if he agrees to it, of course.'

'I think the insurance company might want us to make the barn a bit more secure. Not that some of them are worth much. I've no idea when he uses that clapped-out white van.'

'Perhaps when he doesn't want to be recognised. Like a disguise.' Then her eyes sparkled as she walked back to the red car. 'Do you think Justin would let me drive this sometime?' she asked, moving her fingers gently over the shiny metal surface.

Rae took a key from her pocket. 'Like now, you mean?' she said, a mischievous look on her face. 'Go on, he needn't even know.'

Shaking her head and pursing her lips, she replied, 'I'm tempted, but I couldn't do that. Maybe I'll ask him later.'

'At least you could sit in it,' suggested Rae, opening the door.

Thea was tempted, but shook her

head. The last thing she needed was to get into Justin's bad books. 'Thanks, Rae, but the answer's still no.' Rae reluctantly put the key back in her pocket. Thea strolled round the rest of the barn, stopping several times to admire the vehicles.

Noticing something at the back of the barn, Thea asked, 'Is that Justin's motorbike?' She could imagine him taking to the open road on it, roaring around the countryside. No one would recognise him in his helmet, so he could be as free as the wind.

Rae tugged at her hair. 'It's mine,' she said. 'Justin won't let me ride it, says it's far too dangerous. I told him if he got rid of it I'd move out! I do sneak off on it sometimes though when he's away.' She and Thea exchanged an understanding grin. 'Around the village I mostly use that bike.' She pointed to an ancient, sturdy contraption with a large basket on the front. 'Sometimes I take the 2CV.' She shrugged. 'I've never been that into cars.'

★ ★ ★

Thea had begun to think they'd never visit Grace. When Justin arrived home, he took a hunk of bread and went upstairs saying he had some calls to make. Eventually he came back having changed into cream chinos and a Hawaiian top. He plucked at it and explained. 'Grace likes bright colours. I thought this would cheer her up.' He glanced at Rae as she came into the room. 'What're you up to, Rae? Off out somewhere?'

'I'm coming with you,' Rae said.

'Hey,' gasped Justin, looking surprised, 'you look . . . sort of different.'

Rae frowned, 'Oh? In what way?'

Thea lightly touched her arm. 'In a good way, Rae. Let us have a good look at you, please.'

Rae stood, shoulders rounded, a hand on one hip, staring into the distance. 'Hurry up, then, we've got things to do today.'

Thea looked at the young woman's hair which was sparkling with some spray-on highlights, giving her a magical elfin look. She was wearing make-up which, while it had been applied a little heavily, brought her features to life. Around her neck hung a string of sparkling beads and she was dressed in an embroidered gypsy top and cornflower-blue handkerchief skirt. A skirt? Rae in a skirt? Thea cast her eyes down to the ground and saw peep-toed sandals through which gleamed iridescent silver varnish. 'You look gorgeous, Rae. Absolutely stunning.'

Rae looked at her brother. 'Tell her to back off, Justin, it's only me.'

'But she's right. You do look stunning.' He smiled at her and gave her a little punch on the shoulder.

Rae blushed and ducked her head, smoothing her hands down her skirt self-consciously. Then she held up the floral arrangement in front of Justin. 'Aren't these beautiful?'

'Yeah, they are. Did you have them delivered? We could have picked some up on the way.'

'Thea and I chose them from the garden.' She pushed them close to Justin. 'Here, smell that.' Playfully she thrust the bunch into his face. 'Go on, smell them.' As he tried to get away, Rae followed him, poking him with the offering intended for Grace.

Justin finally grabbed her wrist and inhaled deeply. 'What've you got in there? Smells, I don't know, a bit different from flowers. Anyway, Grace will love them. Just one thing. We won't mention the Bakers' visit here, right? Let's go, shall we?'

They left the house. The limo purred up the drive and came to a halt by the front steps. Toby got out, wearing a tomato-red t-shirt and bleached-out jeans. Everyone was making an effort for Grace.

'Hi,' called Thea. She was excited now at the thought of another trip in the limo. Toby appeared incredibly laid-back and kept himself to himself, but she felt he was the sort of person you could totally rely on.

'All three of you going, eh?' he asked.

'That's it, Toby,' said Justin, holding the back door open for Thea. About to wriggle across to the middle seat, Thea was surprised to see Rae open the front passenger door and slip into the seat next to Toby. The magic button was pressed and the glass partition opened between the front and rear seats.

Thea enjoyed looking out at what she took to be Justin's grounds, and then they raced along the motorway. No one spoke, it was as though they were all on edge because of this visit to Grace. She decided to break the silence. 'Does Grace know you're bringing me?' she asked Justin. 'I wouldn't want to be in the way. I can always wait outside if it's all too much for her.'

'She'll love to see you. A new face.' He grinned at her. 'A *pretty* new face.'

Thea felt her cheeks burning and turned away to look out of the window once more.

'Don't look now, but we appear to have the paparazzi on our tail. Hold on

tight if you want me to lose them.'
Toby's eyes kept flicking to the rear
view mirror.

'When did you notice them?' asked
Justin.

'Not long after we hit the motorway.'

'Okay, don't worry about trying to
lose them. But I'll get the registration
number.' Justin turned in his seat then
tapped the numbers into his phone.
'Right, got it. Strange car for the
paparazzi.'

'Yeah, it's an old estate. Weird. They
usually have something a bit more
zippy. But they're a funny lot, you just
never know.'

They continued in silence.

Thea wasn't sure what to expect of
the day, but she hadn't anticipated the
large country house they came up to,
soon after turning off the road.

Toby breathed a sigh of relief. 'They
haven't followed us in.'

Thea felt the tension vanish. 'Is this
Grace's house?'

'She has an apartment in it. The

other residents are similar to Grace, in need of a bit of TLC. Rae and I thought she'd like the company.'

Toby spoke to Justin as he opened his door. 'I'm going to sit in the car, keep an eye on things. Just in case. I'll ring your mobile if the paparazzi turn up and then we can decide how to handle them before you leave the building.' As Thea walked away she heard Toby continue in a whisper, 'I'm sure it wasn't the paparazzi, I just said that so the women wouldn't be alarmed. I can't work out who it was.'

Thea didn't think Rae had heard this exchange because she had already dashed up to the front door and punched in a code. The door swung open and Thea, Justin and Rae went through to a reception desk. Thea looked back worriedly and saw Toby unfold a newspaper. She supposed that if you lived in Justin's type of world you got used to odd situations and accepted them.

'Grace will be pleased to see you,'

said the receptionist, as they signed themselves in. 'Shall I buzz up and tell her you've arrived?'

'If you like,' said Justin. 'She knows we're coming, but she may prefer it if she's prepared for us.'

Grace had her front door open by the time they'd gone up in the lift and along the corridor. 'How lovely,' she said, her eyes shining as she looked at her brother and sister. 'Rae, you look especially nice today. Let me look at you. You've got legs, I see,' she giggled. 'It suits you. Now you've gone pink and I've embarrassed you. I've made some biscuits. Come on in.' Then she seemed to remember that there was a third member in the visiting party. 'Goodness, how rude you'll think me,' she said, extending her hand towards Thea. 'You're Thea, Justin told me that. You're very welcome and it's good of you to visit me.'

'The pleasure's mine,' smiled Thea, holding Grace's small and cool hand.

Grace ushered her in. 'Let me show

you around. It's a cosy little flat and I love being here.'

The narrow hallway led into a living area pleasantly furnished with a sofa and two easy chairs. Under the bay window was a table with a display of framed photos. Off the living area was a small kitchen which had been thrown into disarray with Grace's baking.

'I've got two bedrooms, so that if either Rae or Justin want to stay, I can put them up.' Grace smiled at her brother and sister. 'Toby stays sometimes,' she added.

The afternoon passed pleasantly. The ginger biscuits Grace had baked were delicious. Her thin, pale cheeks flushed as she was praised. 'You can take some home if you like. I've got a bagful for Toby. I wonder why he didn't come in. You know I always like to see him.' She got up and hugged her sister. 'Come with me and have a look at what I've bought over the internet. You stay here, Justin, you won't be interested, it's clothes.'

Thea didn't like to intrude upon the sisters so remained in the room with Justin. She stayed silent as he appeared to be deep in thought. Instead of chatting, she tried to think how the profile could show what a caring and kind man he was. Glancing back at Justin, she saw that he had slipped down in his chair and was fast asleep, a little smile on his full lips. He grunted softly and turned his head, but his eyes remained closed. Thea went to the kitchen and tidied it. She was pleased to have met Grace and wondered what her medical problem was, as she'd appeared happy and well today.

Justin woke up when the sisters returned from the bedroom. Grace said, 'You do love me, don't you, Justin?' She sounded like a child, poor thing, thought Thea.

Justin said, 'Of course I love you. I told you so at two o'clock this morning, didn't I? I wouldn't have answered your call at that time if I didn't love you, would I?'

'You're a dear, and you Rae. And it's lovely to meet you, Thea. Come on, Rae. Let's put those flowers in a vase. I can smell rosemary.' She buried her nose in the blooms and inhaled deeply before grabbing her sister's hand, pulling her to the kitchen.

Justin turned to Thea and said quietly, 'She's so unpredictable. We never know if we're going to be well received or not. She lives a life that we don't understand. On the surface, everything's normal, like her buying those dresses or whatever and baking, stuff like that. But you heard her asking if I love her. She needs constant reassurance or she gets very depressed, not just down, but really depressed. When she phoned in the middle of the night, I thought she was going to say not to come, but she didn't, she just wanted me to tell her I love her. Which I did, of course.' He put his head back on the upholstery.

Thea was sorry for the Anderson family, but having found out that it was

Grace she'd heard Justin talking to in the middle of the night, she was very pleased for herself.

Grace and Rae returned with a vase brimming with the flowers, which Rae placed on a side table.

'I'd love to grow something,' Grace said as she fiddled with one of the flower stems. 'The gardener has been making new beds in the grounds and we've been told we can have one so long as we look after it properly. What do you think? Oh, Justin, wouldn't it be fun? I could grow herbs and all sorts of flowers.'

'It wouldn't be too much for you?'

'Not at all. And I've found some interesting recipes for things like lavender cake, lemon basil snaps and rosemary bread.'

'You're making my mouth water. Shall we go to the garden centre now?' Justin offered.

'I don't feel like going out. There'd be a lot of people and I feel tired. Would you get some things for me? I'll make a list.' Grace found a notebook, sat down and wrote a list with an air of intense concentration. When she had finished she tore the sheet out and handed it to Justin. 'It doesn't matter if you don't get everything on there. And I don't need you to buy tools, I'll use the ones that are here. Now tell me what you've been up to.' She smiled at Rae, 'Are the donkeys and horses getting better? Have you rescued anything else?' Grace leant forwards.

'I took some pigs from an awful family called the Bakers. Pigs are so adorable.'

Grace frowned as though she was trying to recall something. Her mood had changed. 'Thanks for visiting. It's probably best if you go now. I think I'll come down and see Toby if that's all right.'

'Sure,' said Justin. 'Are you going to put some shoes on?'

At last they were ready and Grace almost ran to Toby. 'Here are some biscuits for you. You should have come in. Oh, it's so lovely to see you.'

'You, too, Gracie.'

'You'll be all right getting back up to your flat?' asked Justin, concern filling his face. 'Shall I come with you?'

'Of course I'll be all right,' chided Grace. 'I'm not a child.' Thea was relieved to see Toby follow her as she ran up the steps. Unexpectedly Grace rushed back to the car. 'I've remembered. I knew there was something. It's the Bakers. I've read about them in the local papers being taken to court for different offences. You mustn't cross them. I have a horrible feeling they could be very violent.'

6

'What was Grace saying about the Bakers?' asked Toby. 'Sorry, Justin, I know it's nothing to do with me, but she looked so agitated.'

Justin leaned forward and told Toby what Grace had said. Rae dug into her pocket and brought out her smartphone. 'Here, this might have been what Grace meant. The Baker brothers have a very sordid background. Breaking and entering, robbery with violence, GBH, there's a whole lot of evil stuff here. Yippee is all I can say as it will strengthen our case against them, don't you think?' She looked imploringly at her brother.

'Possibly, Rae, but please try and be a bit more objective about things.' Justin sounded tired and exasperated.

'It says that they've been in trouble with the police for most of their lives.

There's stuff here about driving without a licence and causing an affray in a local pub. I wonder which one that was,' Rae continued, taking no notice of Justin's plea.

Thea observed that Toby kept his eyes on the road, but his facial muscles tightened.

'Relax, Toby, she's not in any danger. She's only read about them in the papers.' Justin put his hand on Toby's shoulder. 'I think you should change the subject now, Rae. There's nothing we can do.'

'Did my brother tell you about our kitchen being trashed?' asked Rae. 'That was the Bakers.'

'Why didn't you say something, Justin?' asked Toby. 'What are you going to do about it?'

'Nothing. Just leave it, will you.'

Rae stared out of the window, her mouth in a pout. Thea hid a smile as she imagined Rae as a child, scolded by her big brother. But the situation wasn't at all amusing.

As Toby pulled up to the house Justin said, 'I'd like to go to the garden centre now, Toby. I know Rae won't want to come. What about you, Thea? Want to see what it's really like being a star?'

Thea couldn't imagine that much out of the ordinary could possibly happen at a garden centre, but the thought of spending more time with Justin appealed, so as soon as Rae had climbed out of the car they set off.

And to start with, it seemed like a normal shopping trip. At first only a few people pointed and stared, but gradually more and more people noticed Izaak Flanagan was in the store.

A middle-aged woman approached. 'Hi, Izaak, can I have your autograph, please?' But as soon as Justin had obligingly signed that one, other people were coming up asking not just for one autograph for themselves, but for friends and family as well.

'Look, Thea, I'm sorry, if I give you the list can you see if you can get the things and load up the trolley?' Justin didn't look angry or upset, just rather wistful.

As Thea walked away with the trolley she turned to see Justin mobbed by people. One woman was hugging him and squealing, 'Look at me! Take my photo, Em.'

Another woman was shrieking, 'It's my turn.'

The sooner they got the things on Grace's list and were back home again, the better. She chose lavender and rosemary plants for outside and also an attractive window box which Grace could put outside her sitting room. Then she selected a pretty planter and herbs for the kitchen.

She gave a sigh of relief when they were both back in the car, their purchases stowed in the boot.

'I don't know how you can stand it, Justin. Why don't you tell them you're out on private business and to leave you alone?'

'I can't do that, can I? Think about it. If I was offhand to my fans I'd soon be out of work. It comes with the territory as they say. What? Why are you giving me a funny look?'

Thea held a tissue towards his face. 'May I? Someone has given you a kiss and left Cranberry Smooch on your cheek.' She wiped his face and suddenly felt embarrassed and looked down at her lap.

Justin stared out of the window and said, 'People always want to get too close to me.'

For the rest of the journey they didn't speak.

They went into the house and Justin said to Thea, 'There's something we've got to discuss.'

She saw his set face and wondered what was up. 'Is it about the interview?' asked Thea.

'Sort of.' Annoyingly, Justin busied himself in the kitchen, moving things around randomly. 'Let's go into the sitting room.'

The sitting room was lovely and Thea was only too happy to spend time there, but what was up?

'I think you're getting a bit too close to the family,' said Justin.

'Right . . . I'll leave, then,' replied Thea, horrified that her acts of kindness had been turned against her. She was sure something was troubling Justin — he seemed to blow hot and cold. Despite what he said, Thea found him a very difficult man to get close to.

'You know I don't want you to leave before we've sorted out what's going to be in the piece and what locations you're going to film.'

Thea sat down in one of the squashy armchairs. 'What do you want, then?' There was no need for a row. She'd nearly finished her work here anyway. All it needed was Justin's approval, which he'd more or less given the day before.

Justin paced the room, a frown marring his perfect features. 'I don't know,' he confessed. 'I want to protect my sisters, is that so wrong?'

'Of course it's not wrong,' confirmed

Thea. 'We're not going to say anything defamatory about them.'

'The fact that they're mentioned at all is enough. I shouldn't have let it happen.'

Thea was confused. 'Rae asked me to get something on TV about the Bakers. How can I do that without involving Rae? I didn't want to do it at first, but she persuaded me to. I've already got the go-ahead from my boss.' Then she understood. Tenderly she said, 'You're afraid they'll get hurt, is that it?'

Justin came and stood in front of her and held out a hand. Thea took it and felt the warm, soft flesh. She didn't want to be sent back home, she wanted to stay here with Justin. She engaged all her senses and let herself be lifted upright and enveloped by him. Without any thought, her arms went around him and she breathed his scent. Then she was aware of his arms around her and his lips kissing the top of her head. She turned her face slightly and their two eager mouths came together, swamping

Thea with feelings she never knew she possessed.

Rae's strident tones caused them to spring apart seconds before she entered the room. 'I'm just going to check on Milly. Last time I looked in on her she was causing havoc down there. She only does it to get attention.' She peered at Justin. 'You okay? You look a bit . . . funny.'

'Of course I'm okay. Don't go on, Rae.'

'Pardon me,' she said, raising her eyebrows at Thea.

In order to change the subject, Thea said, 'I've been telling Justin that my boss is keen to go ahead with the story of the Bakers and their nasty ways.'

'Good,' smiled Rae. 'Well done, you. It's good you're here.'

Was it good she was there? Thea asked herself. On several levels it was, but she was on a rollercoaster as far as her feelings were concerned. Perhaps it would be better to get on with things, keep a low profile and get out of the house back to London. 'Justin, you said you'd looked at the questions for the interview. You seemed to think they were all right. Shall we just run through it again. Then I can get back home?'

'You sound anxious to leave,' he said, his penetrating gaze making Thea distinctly uncomfortable as she didn't know what to do or say.

'Hey, give the girl a break, Justin,' put in Rae. 'She's held the house together these last few days. And she's a big hit with the animals. With the possible exception of Milly, but then Milly is always stubborn.'

'Let's have another look at your questions, then,' said Justin. 'But I warn you I'm not really in the mood at the moment. It's been a long day, a lot's happened.'

You can say that again, Thea told herself. Then she trailed upstairs to get the notes.

She lingered on the landing, admiring the paintings. They were exotic in their colour, yet obviously still lifes or landscapes, a combination which made them almost surreal. She was already familiar with the fields in the paintings, and she grinned even though her heart was heavy. She could almost hear and smell Milly, expecting her to pop out from the shelter if she waited long enough. But both Justin and Milly now appeared to be united in their view of her. If Justin wanted her to go, why had he kissed her? Was it a farewell kiss? Involuntarily, her fingers traced an outline around her mouth, trying to conjure up the moment Justin's lips had met hers. Her body was way ahead of her and did its own remembering.

Hearing a door opening on the ground floor, Thea ran lightly up the stairs to her room, where she shut the door firmly. She took a couple of deep breaths, re-read the interview and then packed her case. Now she knew what to do: run away. Run away? Was that what she was doing? Her usually clear mind was misty. One step at a time had always been her mother's advice. Deciding against changing into mucking-out gear, she brushed her hair, applied lip gloss and forced a smile, before darting down the stairs again.

'Here it is,' she called, as she entered the sitting room. 'It's still the same as when you looked at it before.' She held out the sheaf of paper to Justin. Rae was nowhere to be seen.

Thea waited impatiently while Justin flicked through the pages, nodding from time to time. When he got to the last page, Thea had to grit her teeth as she waited for him to speak first.

Eventually, he said, 'This is fine. What do I do? Sign it?'

'Why are you being so distant, Justin? I came here at your kind invitation. I could have done the interview any-where, on a park bench, even. Agreed it's better to have seen where you live and what you do when you're not in the spotlight, but then you . . . we . . . got close. As soon as you'd kissed me just now, you backed off. What's going on?' Thea felt she'd put herself on the line, but it was just what her heart told her. Only she'd never known before how much she could be overtaken by the emotions she'd experienced — was still experiencing. She looked at him and saw — not a film star with stunning looks and a fantastic body — she saw the man she was falling in love with and didn't want to leave. She also felt he was trying to cover up his feelings for her. Why would he do that? Because he had someone else, she told herself; that could be the reason. She'd already asked him if there was a special person in his life, but he hadn't answered.

'I asked you here because I thought it would be easier for us both. You've been a very big help, but don't get the idea that we need you here. We managed all right before you came and we can manage again now.'

'Well thanks for the slap in the face.' Thea felt tears threatening and grew cross with herself. She would not cry. Anger made her retort, 'You could afford to have paid help, you didn't need to rely on me doing it for nothing.' One look at Justin's face told her she'd said the wrong thing. It was said in bitterness and she couldn't take it back, but she wished with all her might that she could. Growing unexpectedly afraid of what Justin might do or say, she stood up and marched towards the door. 'Forget the interview. I don't want it. I can't be bothered to play these games.'

She stalked out, back up the stairs to her room, feeling very glad that she'd already packed, but very annoyed with herself. The situation could have been handled a lot more maturely. Did she really want to scurry away from Justin? More than anything, she wished he had come after her or said something to indicate he would miss her. To be fair, she hadn't actually given him a chance, had she? Just ranted and fled.

Bumping her luggage down the stairs, she desperately hoped Justin wouldn't be around when she escaped through the front door. One little, tiny bit of her hoped that he would be around — the little, tiny bit growing into an enormously big bit.

Reaching the front door, encountering no one, she remembered the isolation of the house. How would she get home? How would she get *anywhere*? Luck was on her side though, she heard a car engine getting closer. It was the limo and, if she wasn't mistaken, that was Toby in the driving seat. Thea stuck out her thumb, like a hitchhiker asking for a ride. The car drew level with her and the window lowered.

'Hi there, ma'am. Anything I can do for you?'

Toby's reliable demeanour filled Thea with hope that he would help her. 'Can you give me a ride to the nearest station, please? Or anywhere I can get a bus or some sort of public transport.'

Toby looked her up and down, his eyes lingering on her luggage. 'You're going home.' It was a statement.

'My work here is finished.' Thea

attempted a smile. 'Please, Toby.'

'Sure, hop in.' Polite and helpful as ever, he stowed her luggage in the boot. 'Give me a minute, ma'am.' He disappeared into the house.

Waiting, Thea gave the grounds a last look, hoping she'd made the right decision. A man like Justin wouldn't give her a second chance. If only things had been different. Then she recalled she'd promised Rae the interview about the Bakers. She couldn't let her down and she had no way of contacting her. Beating herself up about it, she remembered there was good old snail mail, which would even reach here. Feeling considerably happier, she waited for Toby. At last the front door opened. Thea reached in her bag for some paper to begin a list of things to do; it always made her feel better to be looking forwards rather than backwards.

Abruptly the car door opened and someone got in beside her at the same time as Toby clambered into the driving seat. She squinted at the other passenger, hoping it would be Rae. It was Justin. Had he come to carry her back across the threshold?

Justin sat impassively beside Thea. He held out a large brown envelope. 'Your hard copy. It's no use to me.' Then he got out of the car and stood on the gravel drive, waiting for Toby to drive off.

'Okay, ma'am?' asked Toby. 'Ready to go?'

'Yes,' replied Thea. 'Ready.'

Toby started the engine and the car regally rolled off. Thea gave a backward glance she hoped neither of the men would see. Justin was still there, too far away for her to make out the expression on his face. What had she done? She hadn't even given him a chance to explain. Gazing down at the brown envelope, she felt tempted to throw it out the window. Something made her look inside and when she did, she read on the first page of the notes: 'Interview by Thea Stafford'. Squinting at the small writing following hers on the page, she saw: 'a beautiful woman who makes me feel human'. That was definitely not in her handwriting. 'Stop the car. Go back,' she yelled, her hand flying to the door handle.

The emergency stop Toby performed was in the first class category. He was ready for it, she wasn't. While Toby completed the one hundred and eighty degree turn, Thea scrabbled for her poise from the floor of the roomy car. When Justin opened the door of the car, Thea tumbled out at his feet.

'Forget something?' he asked as he extended a helping hand to haul her upright.

Not knowing how to deal with the situation, Thea was at a loss for words. If this were a romcom, she'd have said, 'Yes, this . . . ' and then given him a passionate kiss before they strolled off into the sunset. Then she remembered that it was a passionate kiss which had started all this bad feeling between them. As it was, the best she could come up with now was, 'I just wanted you to know that I'll be in touch with Rae about the Bakers.' From the heat of her face, she knew she had gone an ugly crimson. Infuriatingly, Justin was smirking, his dimple mesmerising her.

'I'll pass on your message,' he assured her, still holding onto the car door handle. 'Are you getting back in or what?'

'Um, yes, I suppose I should. And thanks for your hospitality.' She stuck out a hand towards him which he took and held onto.

'Why exactly are you going? I can't remember.' He appeared to be teasing her.

With an unsteady voice, she said, 'I'm not sure myself now.' Feeling an idiot, with tears brimming her eyes, she looked down at the drive and felt her way back into the car.

Justin hopped in beside her again. 'Please, Thea, I didn't mean to upset you or take you for granted. I'm sorry. We did have a housekeeper, but she wasn't very honest and things went missing. And I haven't got round to getting back to the agency.' He caught at her arm. 'Come back in, stay a while longer.'

'I'm not sure,' she sniffed. 'I'm not sure of anything anymore.'

As if steering a child across a busy road, Justin led Thea back into the house. She was vaguely aware of him gesturing to Toby, probably to get her luggage out of the boot. With Justin's hand gripping hers, Thea realised she hadn't been entirely truthful to Justin. She was very sure of one thing, and that was her growing feelings for him.

Thea was expecting to be taken into the kitchen, but to her surprise they were heading for the sitting room. For some reason her thoughts returned to the paintings and flowers on the first landing and she asked Justin about them.

Now it was his turn to go pink right to the tips of his beautifully shaped ears. 'I did the paintings,' he admitted.

'What do you think of them?'

'I'm not an expert, but I like them.'

'Thanks. Shall I get you some tea, or would you prefer a glass of wine?'

Deciding to relax and take time to calm down, she said, 'Wine, please.'

Handing her a full glass, Justin sat beside her. 'I shouldn't have asked you to go. Every time I see Grace I realise just how vulnerable our tiny family unit is. As a man in the public eye, I have to be careful of scams against my sisters. A beautiful woman is often used as a decoy for me to be trapped by. Of course I trust you. You've been wonderful and I like your interview. I understand why you've had to include Rae, but could we keep the topics separate, please?'

Digesting all this, and taking a gulp of wine, Thea said, 'Good idea. If I can find my notes I'll make some changes.'

'They'll be with your case in the hall. Toby brought in your things.'

'He's very dependable. Grace likes him, too,' remembered Thea.

'They went out together,' admitted Justin. 'But she couldn't bear him being away sometimes for days on end. In the early days, he used to drive me everywhere and was a good bodyguard.'

'Isn't he now?' Thea was intrigued.

'Do I look like I need a bodyguard?' Justin menacingly flexed his muscles. Thea giggled and Justin frowned. Then a grin lit up his face. 'If you're staying, will you let me take you out later this evening?'

Thea choked on the wine. 'What, you mean like a date?'

'Yeah, like a date.' Justin had the whisper of a smile on his lips and a twinkle in his eyes. 'And don't give me any rubbish about your wardrobe. Anything you've got will be fine.'

'But . . . '

Justin patted her lightly on the knee. 'No buts.' With that he got up and left the room.

Thea was aware that once again Justin hadn't said a time or where they were going. Also, more pressingly, she only had strawberry-red trainers to go with her little black number. She was a bit annoyed with herself for not having packed some strappy sandals which would have made her look more stylish. Finishing the wine, she traipsed upstairs with her luggage.

It had been a strange and interesting day and Thea felt she'd learnt a lot, not only about Justin, but also his family. She was over the moon with the fact that she and Justin were going on a date. She half thought he was joking, but she wasn't going to go there. If nothing else came of this outing, she was jolly well going to make sure she revelled in the fact that she was going to spend an evening with Justin Anderson. Hoping a shower would clear her head so that she would be on top form for later, she headed for the bathroom. As warm water cascaded around her, she lifted her head into the stream and rubbed oils into her skin.

Then she wrapped herself in a large, fluffy towel, brushed her hair and dried it roughly before allowing herself a smile of contentment.

A light knock on her bedroom door roused Thea from a doze she'd fallen into after collapsing on the bed. 'Who is it?' she mumbled.

'Me,' called Justin. 'No need to open the door. I'll meet you in the sitting room around eight. Oh, and please don't worry about Rae. She's going to eat with friends this evening after she's sorted out the animals.'

Then Thea heard his footsteps continuing along the landing. A brief glance at her watch told her she had time to continue her nap. Turning over and letting out a long sigh, she tried to recapture her dream.

★   ★   ★

Thea woke feeling refreshed. For once her hair had dried into flirty, wavy curls despite being slept on. Smiling as she pulled her little black dress over her head, she only had a second of self-doubt as she pulled on the red trainers. Justin knew her situation well enough.

Slinking down the staircase, she hoped she wasn't too early, but Justin was waiting in the hall. He looked gorgeous in black jeans, cream shirt and . . . she couldn't believe it, red trainers.

'Snap,' he grinned as they drew level with each other.

'Did you have them in your cupboard or did you send out for them?' asked Thea, eyeing the shoes.

'Now that would be telling. I've called a taxi as it's Toby's evening off. It won't be as swanky as the limo, is that all right?'

'Makes no difference to me. I'm glad Toby gets some time to himself.'

'I'm not the ogre employer you think,' said Justin, taking her arm. 'Oh, sorry, it's still sore,' he said, as she winced slightly at his touch.

'It's okay, I'm not a baby,' retorted Thea. 'Where are we going?'

'Wait and see.'

'I've been there before.' Thea giggled as they went out through the front door to the waiting car.

Once in the nearby town, Justin asked for them to be dropped off at The Regent Hotel. Thea noted that he was a good tipper and it certainly hadn't been to impress her as the gesture had been done surreptitiously.

'I thought we could start here,' said Justin, taking Thea's hand and guiding her through the door which was opened by the doorman. 'Thanks, Len. How's the family?'

'Good, thanks, Justin,' returned the doorman. 'Nice to see you again.'

The receptionist gave Justin a broad smile. 'Justin, how are you?'

'I'm fine, thanks, Muriel. We've just popped in for a drink,' he said before they went through to the cocktail lounge.

'Do you know *everyone* here?' asked Thea.

'Pretty much. The staff are good and there's not as quick a turnover as in a lot of hotels.'

A thought occurred to Thea. 'Do you own this place?'

'Some of it,' came the enigmatic reply. 'Now, what do you fancy to drink?'

'A vodka and coke, please,' said Thea, 'with lots of ice.' Thea watched as he started up yet another conversation with the man behind the bar. They laughed together as the drinks were poured.

'Cheers,' toasted Justin. 'When we've had these drinks, you'll have to decide where you'd like to eat.'

'But I don't know the places around here. Why don't you choose?' Thea sipped her drink, enjoying the coldness as the evening had turned warm.

'I know an out of the way place which I hope you'll enjoy.'

For a moment, Thea thought he wanted to be hidden away with her, but then she remembered his celebrity status.

The restaurant was a short walk from the hotel down a side street. Justin was obviously known by the staff, but they treated him no differently from any other visitor as far as Thea could see. It must be difficult for him to go places and continually have people fawning over him or harassing him.

'Shall we have a selection of meze? Or would you prefer separate dishes?' he asked, studying the menu.

'I'm happy to share,' smiled Thea.

Justin took her hand. 'I'm happy that you're sharing with me.'

He ordered wine and the meze. Taking a gulp from her glass gave Thea the courage to ask him, 'Why did you ask me to leave?'

Frowning, Justin replied, 'I don't think I said that exactly, did I? If I remember correctly, I said you were getting too close to the family.'

'Yes, that's right,' said Thea, picking up a fork trying to decide what to try first. It all looked so appetising, especially the prawn saganaki and moutabel. She took some of each and helped herself to some pitta bread. 'It sort of indicated that you didn't want me around.'

Justin sighed and took her free hand. 'I warned you that I was tired. When I'm really on edge and stressed, that's what happens to me. I get extreme. I'm sorry.' He raised Thea's hand to his lips and kissed it. 'I don't want to rely on you. I must look after my sisters as well as carving out my career. Please understand.'

'I think you're being very hard on yourself, Justin,' said Thea, rubbing her thumb along his hand. 'If I can help a little, why can't you just accept it?'

Justin abruptly let go of Thea's hand and ran his fingers over his face. He looked utterly drained. 'Because I've been let down in the past. There have been people who've made me believe they were doing things for me or just being friendly when actually they were either gold-diggers or undercover reporters trying to dig the dirt. I don't trust people.'

'You've got a lovely rapport with all

sorts of people, not just your family, but the staff in the hotel just now and here in the restaurant. You get up early and go to the studio and then have the house and everything to think about, it's an awful load.'

Justin seemed thoughtful. 'You're a sweet woman,' he said, looking a little more relaxed.

'So are you,' replied Thea, taking another slug of wine. 'What? What are you laughing at?'

* * *

'I'm so full I couldn't eat another thing,' declared Thea, some time later, sitting back in her chair. 'That pudding was absolutely delicious.'

'What was it you had again?' asked Justin, the hint of a smile around his lips.

'That custardy thing. Galalaptop. Something like that anyway.'

'Galaktoboureko.' This time his smile was wide and his dimple visible.

'See, you do remember.' Thea narrowed her eyes at him. 'Are you making fun of me?'

'Never!' grinned Justin. 'Anyway, as long as you enjoyed what you had. What shall we do now?'

More than anything Thea wanted to stretch out the evening in his company, but she replied, 'Can we go home, please?'

'Are you sure?'

'Yes, I'm sure. You're tired and I'm . . . well, I'm, that is to say, I think I may have had a little much to drink, I mean . . . '

Justin paid the bill, called a taxi and gently put Thea into the back seat before getting in beside her. The journey wasn't long, but Thea grew sleepy. When they reached the house, Justin helped her indoors and up the stairs.

'Here you are, Thea. Your room.'

Thea tried to focus, but it wasn't easy. She registered where she was and got herself into her room, calling to

Justin, 'Thanks for a nice time.' And then she collapsed onto the bed and fell fast asleep.

* * *

A hefty thump on her bedroom door roused Thea. What was she still doing in her dress and trainers? Then she remembered. How embarrassing was that? Struggling to sit upright on the bed, she heard the hammering again.

'Come in,' she called.

'Thea, what happened to you?' Rae approached the bed and deposited a large mug of tea on the table. 'You look as if you need this? Heavy date was it?'

'I went out with Justin and drank too much. I never drink too much.' Thea sat, feeling forlorn. 'He'll hate me now.'

'Who's going to hate you?' Justin appeared at the open door. 'Morning, Thea. I see you're up and dressed ready for the day.' Then he disappeared into the room housing the computer and shut the door.

153

'Poor Thea,' sympathised Rae, sitting next to her. 'You won't get anything out of him for a while now. He hasn't gone to the studio today. He'll be lost on the computer doing household accounts and other stuff which I usually have to do.'

'He couldn't really have thought I was dressed for the day, could he?' asked Thea. Now why should she care what he thought? Because she'd fallen in love with him, that was why. And she didn't want him to think she was anything less than perfect.

'Drink your tea and have a bracing shower,' smiled Rae, burrowing in the wardrobe. 'Here, these clothes should be all right for today.' She gave Thea a kindly hug and added, 'Can I help?'

Thea shook her head. 'You already have,' she said attempting a smile.

*   *   *

By mid-morning Thea was feeling almost normal. She decided to go and see what she could do to help. The door to the study was still firmly closed and there was no sign of Rae downstairs. She was probably out in the field as usual. The kitchen was in disarray, despite the fact that the cleaning and maintenance company had finished their work. Thea guessed Rae was responsible for the clutter. However, Thea enjoyed putting it right.

Out of habit, she sliced onions and put them in a large saucepan before adding chopped vegetables and some beans.

'Smells good.'

The voice startled Thea and she whirled round, her head thudding in protest at the sudden sharp action. 'Hello, Justin,' she murmured. 'I was just getting on with things.' Thea stopped stirring the contents of the saucepan, but didn't look at Justin although she was aware of him moving around behind her. When he put his hands on her shoulders, she instinctively turned around and lifted her face to his. His mouth found hers and the kiss was long and loving.

'Leave her alone, Justin. I'm starving,' laughed Rae as she entered the kitchen at just the wrong moment. 'I suppose I should have pretended I didn't see you and crept out again. Sorry.'

Certain that her face was as red as her trainers, Thea grimaced as she reluctantly pulled herself away from Justin. 'No problem.' She looked at Justin; she could have stayed in his arms forever. He gave a small wink and left the room.

Rae sat on a kitchen chair and heaved her boots off. 'I'm really sorry, Thea. I didn't realise it was serious with you and Justin.'

'I'm not sure it is,' replied Thea. 'At least not on his part.'

'You've really fallen for him, haven't you? It won't be easy for you because of his fans. I'm surprised the press hasn't got wind of you being here and made something of it.'

'Oh no, I hadn't thought about that,' said Thea, horrified at the idea. 'Looking on the bright side, we do need media involvement for your animals, don't we?'

'Speaking of which, I think Milly's missing you.'

'Bless her, I'm missing her, too.' The two women collapsed in giggles and the mood lightened.

Justin came back into the room. 'There's a possibility I'll have to go to Sweden for a few days. Fancy tagging along?'

'Me?' asked Thea, unsure who Justin was inviting. The idea was appealing. 'I'd love to come.' It would be an adventure, but it mightn't be an easy trip with Swedish fans mobbing Justin. Perhaps she should have told him she'd think about it.

Justin's phone trilled. 'Hi, Toby. What's up?' His face contorted as he listened. He ended the call abruptly and hurried from the room.

7

Thea wondered what could have made Justin rush off without a word. He'd looked furious and she wanted to help. Then she thought back to the previous evening and couldn't help but smile. She'd been on a date with Justin Anderson and he'd invited her to go to Sweden with him. There was no way she could predict the future, but admitting to herself that she had most definitely fallen in love with him, she realised all she wanted was for them to be together. If only she knew how Justin felt about her. Rae interrupted her thoughts.

'What's all that about?' Rae asked. 'Wait a minute, it was Toby who rang, wasn't it? Perhaps one of Justin's precious cars has a problem.' She chewed at her thumb.

'You're obviously worried. Phone him.'

'It's unlike him to go off like that without a word. He looked so angry.' Rae quickly took out her phone and called Justin. 'Hi Justin, we're worried. Phone as soon as you can.' She looked across at Thea, 'I got his voicemail.'

'There's nothing we can do except wait. Let's have some food.' Thea's mind wandered to the night the Bakers had called and threatened Justin with an iron bar. Could it have anything to do with them? Her heart thumped when she thought of the possibility that Justin could be in grave danger. She would have to put on a brave face for Rae, but if anything happened to Justin what would they do? Thea was determined not to take that route. She tried to convince herself that even the Bakers wouldn't be so stupid as to be violent to Justin. They'd be torn apart by the media and his adoring fans, and the way Thea was feeling, she wouldn't be far behind in exacting retribution. She didn't want to imagine Justin being hurt and wished now she'd gone after him when he'd rushed out. She was convinced that if she was with him everything would be all right.

Both young women played with the food on their plates, then Rae let her fork clatter down. 'This is impossible. I'm going to see Milly and co. Want to come?'

Thea watched Rae grooming the horses. It hadn't been a good idea to leave the house. Her feelings were all over the place. Not only was she worried about Justin, she also felt tearful about the cruelty these poor creatures had suffered. They were so trusting and yet their trust had been misplaced. She made her way to the pigs' enclosure and patted them when they came over to her snuffling and grunting. It was surprising how quickly they were getting over their trauma, but she still couldn't believe the misery the Bakers had inflicted on them. Her phone rang and she hurriedly pulled it from her pocket hoping it would be Justin calling. It was Dave.

'Hi, Thea. I need to have some idea of what's going in this piece on those Baker people.'

'I'm outside and haven't got my notes so I can't tell you exactly, but I can give you a pretty good idea. Rae rescued, or stole, the pigs from the Bakers and accused them of cruelty. That's the gist of it, but I'm hoping to dig deeper and find out more about them.'

'Yeah, as I thought. We're going to have to be a bit careful. Some of that could be libellous. Just take it easy, okay. Gotta dash, gotta meeting on the second floor ten minutes ago. Hermione's here and wants a word. I'll pass you over.'

Thea almost groaned out loud.

'Thea, I want you to get down to those Baker people at the very latest tomorrow, this afternoon would be best.' As usual Hermione was giving orders rather than asking.

'I don't get it,' Thea protested, 'Put Dave back on, he didn't say anything about this.'

'He's gone to his meeting. Just remember I'm his deputy, and your boss. We've decided to produce a short documentary on animal cruelty. We need a bit more background about these people before we do any filming. I'll email you some questions.'

'They're not peace-loving hippies, they like violence. I'm not sure I want to go on my own.' Thea didn't want to sound pathetic, but she'd seen the Bakers in action.

'If Dave weren't so busy he'd have told you what was happening. The fact is that we need someone with more experience to oversee the Justin story. You're just a beginner and can't be trust . . . that is, you haven't the skill to do it.'

Thea drew in her breath. This wasn't going well. She was cross with herself for not being able to stand up to Hermione. If only Dave was around. She opened her mouth to answer, but Hermione was still going on.

'The viewers know me, they like me,'

she said, glossing over the truth. 'Thea, if you know what's good for you you'll take what you're given and be grateful. Jobs are at a premium right now, if you catch my drift.'

'What is it that I'm being given then, Hermione?' Thea wanted to know. At least it wasn't the sack, not yet anyway.

'You can do the pig thing. I'm sure you're far more suited to muddy fields and dirty creatures than I am.'

In spite of everything Thea smiled inwardly. If she were honest, she couldn't really see Hermione in muddy boots. But she, Thea, had worked hard on Justin's interview and felt she was being usurped. It wasn't fair! Silence hung between the two women until Thea broke it, saying, 'So you're going to be the presenter for the Justin Anderson piece?'

'I've just said so. Please listen, Thea.'

'I want to be sure. And I'm doing the Bakers' story, is that right? I've got a clear run at that?'

Hermione breathed out hard. 'Of

course it will have to be approved by me first. We can't have you wrecking our reputation when we're doing so well. If you're not happy, I'll do that as well. But just remember you had the chance.'

'Okay, I'll do it.' Just as Thea put her phone back in her pocket, Rae came running over frantically gesturing at her. She was talking to someone on her phone.

'It's just awful. Give Grace my love. Tell her I'll be over to see her soon. Have a quick word with Thea. Bye, Justin.' She handed the phone to Thea.

'What's going on, Justin?' Above all she longed to hear that nothing dreadful had occurred.

'Rae will tell you. I want you to know that everything will be all right. I'm going to keep you, Rae and Grace safe. You all mean so much to me. Must go. Love you.' He hung up and Thea tried to make sense of what he'd said. She passed the phone back to Rae.

'Oh, Thea, I can't believe it. It's

terrible and it's all my fault.' Rae sank her head in her hands.

Thea wrapped her arms round Rae and gave her a hug. 'Please tell me what's going on. I'm really worried. Why did Justin say he was going to keep us safe?'

'It's because of what's happened to Grace, poor Grace. Someone's been in her apartment. While she was resting in her bedroom this morning, she heard noises in the sitting room. Although she was terrified she went in and found two men wearing balaclavas. One was going through her handbag and the other was standing guard. She said he was holding some sort of weapon. One of them pushed her and she fell to the floor before she could cry out. He held his hand over her mouth until the other one said he was ready to go and they ran out. Grace screamed, but she said no one heard so she rang reception. By that time it was too late. They'd got away.'

'Is she hurt?'

'Shaken more than anything. Justin and Toby took her to the hospital to make sure, and now they're all at Toby's place. Justin's furious the men were allowed access, but there was a new member of staff on duty and they bluffed their way in.'

'Let's walk back to the house and you can tell me how any of that can possibly be your fault.'

Thea placed mugs of tea on the table and asked the same question again. 'Now tell me, Rae, how can a burglary at Grace's apartment be your fault?'

'Don't you see? It was the Bakers. It would be too much of a coincidence otherwise.'

'What did they take?'

'She said there was some money in her handbag. She thinks that's all, although she hasn't had a chance to check the whole flat.'

'But why? Why would they do that?'

'To scare us. To show us that they know about Grace. Maybe they think they can get a lot of money from a magazine. The headline will be: 'Heart-throb Justin Anderson locks sick sister in home'. Honestly, you've no idea.'

Both women jumped when the back door opened.

'Hey, you must keep this locked, get security conscious.' Toby walked over to the table. His whole demeanour had changed and Thea thought she wouldn't like to meet him on a dark night in this mood. 'It was them.' He clenched his fists and held them tightly at his sides.

'You're sure, Toby?' Rae jumped up and put her hand on his arm.

'Yep. Remember that car following us when we went to Grace's. Justin took the licence number. I've been down to the Cock and Bull pub in the village and the owner says it's definitely the Bakers' car. They're always in there.'

'That doesn't prove anything though, does it?' Thea asked.

'A car just like that was seen by the gardener at the apartments, hidden away behind some bushes, at the same time as Grace was being robbed. He didn't get the number, but it sounds like the same vehicle, from his description.' Thea could see that Toby was trying very hard to contain his anger as he added, 'I'm going to the police to tell them. If they don't believe me, I'm taking the law into my own hands. I only dropped by because Justin insisted I made sure his favourite women here are all right.' He hurriedly left the room calling, 'Lock the door after me.'

Thea went and turned the key in the lock. She was glad Grace was all right, but was petrified at the thought that she still had to pay the Bakers a visit or possibly lose her job, but at least she could go to the farm and look around secretly.

Rae gulped down her tea. 'I'm going to see Grace. I'll cycle, it's not far to Toby's place. You'll be all right here, won't you? Like Toby says keep everything locked. See you later.'

Thea was relieved Rae had gone. She didn't want to have to take her along to the farm as well. If she just pretended to herself she didn't know anything about the Bakers' visit to Grace, she might be all right. She'd do her best to act normally, although with the thought of everything that had happened she'd deserve an Oscar if she managed that. Already her hands were sweating and she was trembling. 'Pull yourself together, Thea,' she said out loud. The vibration of the phone in her pocket announced the arrival of an email from FPC's solicitor with various warnings about what she should and shouldn't do. A text from Dave suggested she involve the animal rescue people. With a sigh of relief she telephoned and arranged for an officer to meet her at the Bakers' farm. The situation seemed less scary now, but on the other hand she'd have to actually face the Bakers.

Then she allowed herself to dwell for a few minutes on Justin's words to her. He'd said he was going to keep her safe and he'd also said 'love you'. Had he meant anything by that or was it the way he always ended his calls to people he knew? For the moment, she must forget about Justin and whether she meant anything to him and remain focused on the job in hand.

First she had to find the farm on google maps and work out a route and then find some way of getting there. Having printed off a map, she searched the drawers in the kitchen. She knew she was taking liberties and desperately hoped Justin would forgive her. At least her own car insurance covered her to drive any car. Finding a small drawer with a variety of keys she selected the one with the Ford logo. She hoped it would fit the white Ford transit van she'd seen in Justin's barn. There was a padlock key on the same ring, which she rightly assumed fitted the barn door.

It didn't take her long to drive to the Bakers' farm. It was a complete mess with broken-down machinery, plastic bags and rubbish littering the place. An old tumbledown farmhouse stood behind an overgrown garden, and in the yard was a scruffy caravan. She was alarmed when she heard raised voices coming from the other side of the caravan.

'What's going on? What the hell are you doing on our property? Get lost or I'll throw you on the dung heap where you belong.' Unwin glared at Thea.

Thea couldn't find her voice at first, then she said quietly, 'I'm meeting someone from the animal protection people here.'

'What's all the fuss about? It's a few animals, that's all, why should you care? We haven't hurt them.'

'Wilful neglect is abuse.' Thea was relieved to see the officer striding towards them.

'Right, Mr Baker and Mr Baker, here I am again. I've come to check up on you and see if you've done what I suggested last time I was here. I understand that this young lady is making a programme about animal cruelty and you are being co-operative.'

The officer from the animal rescue centre winked at Thea before heading for an outbuilding.

Thea was aghast that there were other animals on the Bakers' premises. If only Justin were here with her; he'd know how to handle things. At the moment she felt frightened and vulnerable. The whole thing was getting too much for her. Now she had to start asking questions and make some notes. Shakily she pulled her notebook from her bag. Act normally, she told herself. Before she could ask her first question, Unwin shook something in front of her face. Taking hold of it she realised it was a photo of a younger Grace holding a baby. Unwin snatched it back.

'You should ask your pretty boyfriend what his sister got up to ten years ago.'

'Don't go telling us what to do when we look after our animals a darned sight better than you lot care for your babies. Go and tell that idiot Justin that we'll need an incentive in order to keep silent, if you know what I mean,' said Unwin.

'Yeah,' added Zach, stepping towards her. 'You tell him that. No one takes our pigs and gets away with it, not even celebs.'

Unwin pushed Zach to one side. 'It's not just our word against theirs. We've got written proof. A letter. Be sure to tell him that.'

Thea had no idea what they were talking about, but she was feeling threatened and decided to cut short her visit. She ran to the van, jumped in and accelerated away.

8

Thea was thankful to get back to Justin's house. She was frightened and longed to find comfort with him. He'd tell her things were going to be all right, wouldn't he? Justin was in the kitchen making tea and shortly afterwards Rae arrived.

'Grace is putting on a brave face. Thank goodness Toby's going to be looking after her. Are you all right, Thea? You look a bit pale,' said Rae.

Thea explained about the call with Dave and Hermione.

'You didn't go to the farm on your own,' said Justin. After Thea had nodded, Justin hugged her tightly. 'I'm glad you're safe.'

She swallowed and said, 'I took the white van without asking, I'm sorry and I hope you don't mind, Justin.'

'That's the last thing I'm worried

about. The insurance would cover you. Why choose that one with all the other classy ones sitting there? Didn't you fancy the red TVR?'

'You had your eye on that one when I showed you all the vehicles, didn't you?' Rae asked.

'Yes, but I thought it was too special to take to the farm. But there's something more important I need to ask.'

'Ask away.'

'Did any of your family have a baby, Justin?'

Justin quirked his eyebrows. 'Funny question. How do you mean?'

Feeling foolish, Thea elaborated. 'One of those awful Baker brothers showed me a picture of someone who looked like Grace, but younger. She was holding a baby. He's got some sort of letter too. He said I had to ask you about it and I think he's got blackmail on his mind.'

Justin shot Rae a look, and they both sat down at the table. Justin's hands were shaking. She wished she could reach out and touch him to give him some comfort. Rae was quiet. No quip came from her this time. It was serious.

Slowly Justin said, 'Grace had a baby, yes. He was put up for adoption because of the rather delicate situation at the time. They must have gone through her desk as well as her handbag. That letter would be the one from the adoption agency. The thing was, Thea, Grace was young and impressionable and she got in with the wrong crowd. Like now, she was always seeking approval from other people and she'd do the most outrageous things in order to be accepted by her peers. She started going to nightclubs, getting in even though she was underage. She got mixed up with a high-profile but sleazy politician and ended up pregnant. When she told him, he acted as if he'd never seen her before. It really cut her up. What with her illness as well, there was no way she could have coped with a baby, and she insisted he was given up for adoption. Our parents saw how distressed Grace was and went along with what she wanted, even though they were heartbroken. Rae and I would have helped with him as well, but Grace was adamant. It was a terrible time.' Justin shuddered before continuing. 'I guess the Bakers think they can scare me into giving them a load of money.' He took Thea's hand and pulled her into the chair next to him. 'Please believe me when I say that I really don't care for myself. Okay, I'll get bad press and will probably lose some film roles. I can live with that. It's Grace and Rae I want to protect. That's all I've ever wanted to do.'

He looked so lost and alone that Thea's heart went out to him. She'd do anything she could to help him get through this. She squeezed his hand. 'I'm not doing the interview with them if it means that your past will come out. If the public hear about Grace, it won't be from me.'

'Thank you, it means a lot that you're

on our side in all this,' said Justin. Rae sat in silence. Justin scraped his chair back and said, 'At least we don't need to worry about Grace's physical well-being as Toby will look after her and I think she finds his company more peaceful than ours. That's families for you. Also the Bakers have less chance of finding out where she is.'

* * *

The dawn chorus woke Thea and she stretched her limbs before leaping out of bed. This was more like it; she felt refreshed by the sleep and ready for anything. Then she remembered the night before. She showered and dressed before going down to tackle the tidying up, hoping she wouldn't have to face anyone just yet. To her surprise the kitchen was clean and uncluttered.

She dug her hands into the pockets of her jeans and looked out of the back-door window. A light shower had left spatters of rain on the glass.

Thinking of the horses and not knowing how they fared in wet weather, Thea grabbed an oilskin hanging near the door and hurried out to the field. She was sure she'd seen in one of Rae's magazines that donkeys shouldn't be left out in the rain because it seeps into their coats.

Milly was her first thought. Although she and Rae had laughed about her, Thea was very fond of the donkey. In fact, she was fond of all of them.

Having chased a wet Milly around the enclosure, Thea was about to give up on her. So much for her earlier loving thoughts. 'I'm warning you, I won't come out again and try to save you from yourself,' she threatened.

'Perhaps she likes the rain. Or just the attention.'

Thea slipped on the muddy grass as she turned around, surprised. 'Justin! I was about to . . . '

'So I see,' he said, coming closer towards her and wrapping her in his arms. 'Are you feeling better?'

She was — now she was with him. How corny did that make her? She nestled her head into his chest and relaxed against him. After a while, she said, 'Aren't you getting wet?'

'Yes,' he said, but didn't move and neither did she.

'What are you two idiots doing? If you're out here you could have made sure Milly was warm and dry even if *you* appear to enjoy getting soaked.' Rae rushed at the wayward donkey taking her by surprise and hurried her under cover where she tethered her on a long rope. 'I'll see to the others then, shall I?'

Still receiving no answer, Rae stomped around attending to the wet creatures.

Thea reluctantly released her hold on Justin. 'I'm sorry, Rae. I came out to do that, but . . . '

Rae looked at her and grinned. 'Something got in the way?'

'You could say that,' replied Thea. 'Now what happens with the pigs? Do they have to be put under cover or do they go into their houses if they want to?'

'Best to put them inside. Their bedding will get wet so we'll have to remember to put down dry stuff later.'

The two women set to work.

'Doesn't look like you need me,' said Justin.

'Okay, you're let off the hook, but only because we can manage everything. I think the horses will be all right if the rain doesn't get too heavy,' said Rae. 'Why don't you go on in and put the kettle on. I'm dying for a cuppa.'

Back at the house they got out of their wet things and Thea padded up to her room. She phoned Dave. 'I'm going to delay the interview with the Bakers,' she said firmly. 'I need to be more sure of my facts.'

She was certain she heard a sigh of relief with the reply, 'Okay, Thea. Good thinking. Don't feel you've got to hurry back. We're on a bit of a roll here. Things are going great. Not that it won't be nice to see you, but you deserve a rest.' Thea was a bit put out that she wasn't missed too much. But it was good that Dave was happy for her to be away from the office for a while longer. More time to spend with Justin. If only she could make him happy. He was so miserable because of this business with Grace.

As she went downstairs again, she heard a commotion outside, but couldn't make out where it was coming from. Justin and Rae weren't in the kitchen. She pulled on some boots and grabbed a coat, making her way towards where she thought the sound was coming from. To her horror she saw that the gate to the field had been propped open and the pigs were nowhere to be seen. The horses were running free. Doing her best to round them up on her own, she whispered soothingly to them. If only Justin was here. Why hadn't she called to him and Rae before leaving the house? How was she going to break the news to Rae that she thought the Bakers had taken the pigs back? The short answer was that she wouldn't tell her yet. If Justin and Rae had heard the disturbance they'd be out here. Although she didn't want to leave the donkeys and horses alone now, Thea knew she would have to.

Thea slid into the driving seat of the white van which she'd used before and had left parked at the front of the house. Arriving at the Bakers' farm and not wanting to be seen until she was ready, she parked in woodland at the back of the property. She crept silently through the damp grass, tree branches flicking rainwater across her face, until she could see into the rear of the property. Even though she knew what was going on, she was shocked to see the filthy pigsties with their dirty straw. Apart from the rain, there was no water that she could see. Despite the short time the pigs had been there, they were already looking sad and forlorn.

Thea's heart broke for the pigs as well as Rae. She wanted to help them more than ever. Entering a large outbuilding, she was intrigued when she discovered a big tarpaulin covering something. For some reason she desperately wanted to know what it was concealing. She wrenched at the filthy cover and gasped when she saw what was underneath. Then she smiled to herself. She thought that what she had discovered would be enough to put the Bakers away in prison for a long while.

9

Thea gave silent thanks to the person who invented mobile phones, and called the emergency services. Hiding behind the door of the outbuilding she kept watch for flashing blue lights. As it was, the arrival of the police was much more low key than she expected. After what seemed like forever, a police car arrived almost noiselessly and two uniformed officers stepped out and looked around. Thea rushed out of her hiding place and dragged them back to the outbuilding, explaining as they walked.

'The Bakers have stolen Justin Anderson's car. Come and look.' She led them to the vehicle which had been hidden under the tarpaulin. 'It's definitely his, see it's a green sports car and the number plate is JUST IN. I've seen it at his house. Not long ago.'

One of the officers was already talking to police headquarters while the other was searching the rest of the building. Returning to Thea and his colleague he said, 'There's quite a haul in here. I know at least some of these vehicles have been reported as stolen. Any idea where the Bakers are?'

Thea shook her head.

'You wait here and we'll go and search. If you see them at all, don't approach them. They can get quite nasty.'

Thea didn't need telling. As she went back to her hiding place behind the door and waited, she realised she really wasn't cut out for this type of thing. She longed for Justin to be there with her.

'Hello.'

Thea nearly jumped out of her skin. Her heart was thumping so loudly she had to concentrate hard on what the policeman was telling her.

'They're not here. They've been arrested at the Cock and Bull. We need a statement. Would you like us to follow you home and we'll take it there? You might feel more comfortable than here or at the station.'

Thea hadn't thought she would be interviewed and felt quite shaken at the prospect. She was usually the one who asked the questions. Now she thought about it, it would be much better to give her version of events back at the house. She couldn't wait to see Justin and Rae.

*   *   *

'Well, I'm off then,' Rae said once Thea had told them why she'd gone to the farm and what she'd found.

'Hold on, Rae, I'll come with you later to fetch the pigs and anything else that needs rescuing from their farm. It's just that I think Thea needs a bit of moral support right now.' Justin poured steaming tea into mugs for the police officers and Thea.

'Of course she does. I'll be fine. I'm

going to give Veronica a ring, she'll have finished her shift and will be more than happy to help. We knew there were other animals on the farm and she's been itching to search the outbuildings. See you.' Rae gave both Justin and Thea a hug then was gone.

Justin was allowed to sit in while Thea gave her statement to the police officers, and she was glad he was there. Now things were officially in the hands of the law, she could relax and she hoped Justin could as well. The police had been in touch with the animal rescue people and given Rae the go ahead to look after the animals temporarily at least. Things were turning out well. With any luck nothing detrimental about Grace would come out, and if it did, who was going to take notice of what a pair of thugs said?

'Phew, what a time you've had staying with us. Any regrets?' Justin put his arm round Thea and gazed into her eyes as she snuggled against him on the sofa, once the police had left.

'I wouldn't say it's been exactly peaceful. I suppose if I were Hermione I'd make the most of all the scoops I've had and put everything I've found out in the profile.'

'But you're not that awful woman. You're . . . you're the most amazing person I've ever met and if you even think about leaving I'm going to have to kidnap you.' Turning her face to his, their lips met as if magnetised. Thea gave herself up to his increasing passion with delight, wanting their embrace to last forever.

Totally oblivious to anything but Justin, Thea didn't hear the tap at the door heralding Toby's arrival.

'Hey, sorry,' he said, backing out again.

Justin pulled away from Thea. 'Toby, come in. How's Grace?'

'Gracie's just fine. It looks as though you two are just fine as well.' Toby grinned at them. 'Rae rang and told her the latest developments. Gracie has been burning to get back to her flat and now that she's heard the news about the Bakers being arrested she's already packing her things. Just thought I'd call in and check you're all right. Wasted trip by the looks of things. I'll be off, then.'

After he'd gone, Thea frowned at Justin. 'What's that all about? I thought Toby and Grace were getting back together. Toby seemed so happy having her to stay.'

'Yes, but some things are not to be. They love each other, but with Grace the way she is, things can't work out for them, not at the moment anyway. It's okay, they've both accepted the situation. Now where were we?' He put his arms around her and drew her to him, kissing her hair and moving his mouth softly round towards hers.

Thea was thrilled to be kissing Justin Anderson — what woman wouldn't be? But something was wrong and her brain was getting mixed signals. She pulled herself away from him. 'Am I kissing Justin or Izaak?' she demanded.

'Does it matter?' Justin's mouth was once again searching for hers.

Thea needed to be sure who she was kissing. 'Is this the real Justin Anderson?' she murmured. 'I won't settle for anything less. He's the one I love.'

'This is definitely the real Justin Anderson. Thank you for finding him.' Their lips met once more.

The door burst open again and Rae barged in. 'Not again! Sorry.'

'No problem, how are the animals?' Thea asked, standing up and smoothing her hair.

'The vet's checking them over right now. Milly seems particularly disturbed by the Bakers' latest visit, but I couldn't see any signs of any physical injury. The vet and I are meeting Veronica at the Bakers' shortly and he's going to check the pigs and any other animals are okay before we bring them back.'

'It's really good that they'll all be saved.' Justin smiled at his sister.

'Yes, and it's all thanks to you, Thea.

Finding Justin's car there was absolutely fantastic. You'll end up being the best ever investigative journalist, or whatever it is you are.' Rae rushed over and gave Thea a huge hug. 'And guess what, Justin?'

Justin groaned. 'What now?'

'I've made a decision. I'm going to set up an animal refuge here. Well, if you agree.' Rae looked slightly shamefaced.

'That's fine by me as long as I don't have to be hands on all the time.'

It was Justin's turn to receive one of Rae's bear hugs. 'You are the coolest brother ever. I love you.' With that she was off, out of the room and heading back outside.

'She's very lucky having you,' Thea said, entwining her hand with Justin's and thinking how lucky *she* was to be here with him. He silenced her by placing his lips lightly on hers and pulling her to him.

★　★　★

Lying in bed the following morning Thea went over the events of the last few days and tried to decide what to do next. After showering and dressing, she called Dave's number and told him what had been going on.

'It's all sounding good,' said Dave down the phone line. 'Get yourself back here and we'll see what we can do with it.'

That wasn't what Thea wanted at all. She wanted to be with Justin. 'I *am* working, I'm trying to find out about the real Justin Anderson,' she reminded Dave.

'I should think you'd have found that out by now, right down to the colour of his underpants,' said Dave. 'I understand you've got the hots for him like all the other damn women.' He laughed. 'I still think it's time you came back. Hermione's itching to get rid of you. I think she sees you as a threat. I've a lot on my plate and I need my up-and-coming young star shining in my office even if she'd rather be with some screen idol in the back of beyond. Sorry, Thea, I know you're supposed to be on leave when you've finished with Justin Anderson, but when you've got a scoop, it's best to run with it. We should strike while the proverbial iron is hot.'

Thea knew she'd have to go back if she wanted to keep her job. Her practical side told her that she couldn't just give everything up for a romance with Justin. They hardly knew each other after all. She'd have to tell Justin and Rae she was leaving. It would have been good to spend time with Justin finding out everything about him: what his favourite flower was, what his last meal would be, where he would choose to spend a holiday, that kind of thing.

'Come and have some porridge,' Rae offered. 'I'm afraid Justin has some bad and good news for you.'

'Rae! Why do you have to mention the bad news? Thea didn't know anything about that. Forget what she's said, Thea, the good news is that the Swedish trip is on. We have to set off first thing tomorrow,' Justin said, grinning.

Thea's heart sank. After the conversation she'd had with Dave she knew she'd have to go back to work or she'd be unemployed. 'I can't go with you, I'm sorry.'

'Of course you can. We'll have a great time when I'm not working.'

'I've got to get back to the office. Hermione wants to get rid of me and I think she's got some hold over Dave.'

'If that awful woman somehow stops you from coming to Sweden I shall refuse to cooperate with FPC. That's it as far as I'm concerned.'

'Please, Justin. You must see that if you do that she'll make sure I get the sack. It won't help me or my career in any way at all.'

Justin reached out and took her hand. 'I'll do whatever you want, but I'm not happy. What is it about this woman? Why is she such a dragon?'

'I'm not sure. I heard a rumour that she was madly in love with some man and he let her down. She hasn't got over it. I think she's so pitiless to stop herself from being hurt again.'

'Do you know who the man was?' asked Rae.

'It could have been someone at work, but I've no idea who.'

'You've talked about Dave. Could it be him?'

'That's ridiculous. Dave has been married forever. He met his wife at school, they married young,' Thea explained.

'Exactly!' Rae was triumphant. 'She fell for a married man. Perhaps she's threatened to tell his wife about the affair if he doesn't advance her career.'

Thea couldn't imagine that Hermione was Dave's type of woman, but maybe she'd been different when she was younger. Then she remembered that the Swedish trip was meant to be the good news.

'And the bad news?' she asked.

'It doesn't matter.' Justin glared at Rae.

'If it involves me, I'd like to know, please,' insisted Thea.

Justin pushed across a printed sheet. 'These were our tickets for a surprise trip to Paris next weekend. But I can't go now because of the Swedish trip, so it's off.' He pushed his bowl away and hurriedly left the room.

'I put my foot in it there, didn't I? Don't worry about Sweden, he's bound to be upset. It will do him good. He's too used to getting his own way.' Rae grinned. 'I'm sure there will be plenty of other opportunities for you to go away together and have a loved up time.'

* * *

After several days back at the office, Thea was exhausted. She'd promised herself a lovely long soak in a bubble-filled bath after watching a bit of TV while she ate a microwaved chicken tikka masala. Flicking through the channels she found a news channel, and decided to catch up with what had been going on in the world. Her heart sank as she watched the report. The item showed Justin leaving a fashionable restaurant with a willowy blonde clutching his arm. Then there was a picture of the same woman wearing a revealing evening dress holding on to him at a film awards ceremony, and yet another at a party. Thea jabbed the standby button as tears welled in her eyes. He hadn't wasted much time in finding a replacement.

Perhaps she should have gone to Sweden with Justin and dared Dave to fire her. Given a straight choice she'd choose Justin, of course she would. It was too late now. All she could do was immerse herself in her work and hope there would be no more headlines about Justin to distract her.

Every time her phone rang, Thea hoped that it would be Justin getting in touch, but it never was. Not even a single, little, tiny text from him. For all his protestations that he wanted her to be with him in Sweden, he couldn't even be bothered to phone her. Well, she got the message, but dealing with it was a different matter.

* * *

With the report on the real Justin Anderson eventually lodged with Dave and awaiting his approval, Thea started planning the programme about the Baker brothers. It was a story which needed telling, but she could have done without the reminder of the Anderson family. Her phone buzzed with a message. Grace was letting her know that the herbs were flourishing and she'd like to see Thea again.

Without hesitation, Thea replied that she'd love to visit.

* * *

'You found me without Toby to drive you,' laughed Grace. 'Come in.' She led Thea straight through to the kitchen and gestured towards the window sill. 'Look, perfect herbs.'

'You've green fingers, Grace,' praised Thea. 'I can't even grow weeds.'

'I'm sure you can,' replied Grace, seriously. 'Let's sit down and I'll confess.'

Thea was intrigued as she followed Grace into the living area. 'What have you been up to?'

'Getting you here under false pretences. I really wanted to talk to you about Justin, not herbs,' Grace admitted. 'That brother of mine should be hanged, drawn and quartered. I love him dearly, but he's a flipping nuisance. What was he thinking of in Sweden? He showed himself up dreadfully.'

'He only had a bit of fun,' said Thea, although that wasn't exactly how she'd thought of it at the time or since. She shrugged. 'You can't blame him for that.'

'But he had no right to do it.' Grace was tight-lipped. 'It's obvious how he feels about you. Even a blindfolded pigeon could see he's in love with you.'

'I thought so at one time, but then I decided I'd got my wires crossed. Don't worry, Grace, I'll get over it.' But she knew she never would. Soulmates come along only once in a lifetime and her chance had come — and gone. 'I'm very pleased to have got to know you and Rae, though. I hope we can still be friends.'

'Are you continuing with the piece about Justin?'

'It's going ahead, yes, but one of the senior presenters is taking over the arrangements. She thinks I'm not up to it. I've got to concentrate on the Bakers' story.'

'Heavens! I'd be really intimidated by that.'

'You think I'm not?' smiled Thea. 'As soon as I leave you I'll have to get on with it. I suppose I'm being silly to feel overwhelmed. I probably won't come across the Bakers, I'm just hoping their solicitor will talk to me and some of the local people like neighbours and fellow customers at the pub. If Toby was coming with me I'd feel a lot stronger. How pathetic is that?'

'Toby has that effect on people. Justin, too, if I'm honest. Rae and I depend on him a great deal, always have.' Grace reached out and took Thea's hand. 'Would you like to stay here for a couple of nights? You've got to be around the area, haven't you? You can't very well go to Justin's now.'

'Before I left home I threw some things into a bag as I knew I'd have to find somewhere to book into near here, but I don't want to be in your way. You're used to your own company, and I'm not very sociable at the moment.'

'Please stay. It would be fun for me.'

About to refuse, Thea saw the sense in it. 'I'd love to, Grace. Thank you.' She bent forward and kissed her on the cheek.

The two young women enjoyed preparing a meal using some of Grace's herbs. Just as they were settling down to eat, the doorbell rang. After speaking into the intercom, Grace turned to Thea. 'It's Justin.'

Thea felt betrayed. 'I thought you'd invited me because you wanted to see me, not to set up some sort of meeting with Justin. Isn't there anyone else available to massage his ego?'

'Honestly, Thea, I had no idea he'd appear this evening. Please believe me.' She went to answer the knock at the door.

Thea could hear the conversation. 'How could you turn up like this?' Grace asked angrily.

'Why? Are you having a cosy night in with Toby?' He chuckled, but on entering the room his face lit up. 'Thea!'

Grace stood behind Thea's chair and put her hands on her shoulders. 'I asked Thea to visit me because I like her and I want her to be my friend. If you choose to be unkind to her that's your loss. Thea, tell me you believe I didn't know Justin was coming.'

Thea could hear the tears in her

voice and patted Grace's hand. 'I'm sorry I doubted you. It's just that I don't know who to trust anymore.' She glared at Justin who looked puzzled.

'Our meal's getting cold, Justin. I think you'd better go,' Grace said.

Thea was surprised Grace was being so harsh to the brother she depended on so much.

'I meant to call, Thea, but I didn't have a minute to myself.' Justin sat down at the table. 'I'm sorry you're angry with me, but I did think about you, more than you can imagine.'

Thea was determined she wasn't going to succumb to his charms again. She helped herself to some herb salad then tucked into the roast vegetable lasagne she and Grace had prepared.

'Oh, for goodness' sake. What's wrong? I'm not leaving until you tell me. *And* I'm going to join you, I'm starving.' He went into the kitchen and returned with a plateful of lasagne, and cutlery. 'I'll help myself to wine, then, shall I?'

Grace picked at her food while Thea

and Justin tucked in. When they'd finished the first course, Grace collected the plates and went to the kitchen to fetch the plum clafoutis from the oven.

'Don't be selfish and spoil Grace's meal,' Thea hissed.

'*Me* spoil it! You're the one being childish. I don't know what I've done to upset you, but I'm staying here until I get an explanation. I'll have to stay the night because I've had a glass of wine.'

'Call Toby.'

'It's his day off.'

'Call a taxi.'

'This is ridiculous, Thea. We sound like two silly children.'

Thea relapsed into silence.

With the dessert finished and coffee made, Grace suggested to Thea they watch a romcom. Settling down together on the sofa, they pretended Justin wasn't there and eventually he wandered off.

Thea and Grace wept and laughed through the film until the happy-everafter end.

'That was such fun, Thea. It's lovely to have a friend over.'

Thea agreed. She stretched and yawned. 'I'll be off to bed now, Grace, if you don't mind. I'll try not to disturb you in the morning.'

'I don't usually get up early, but you've given me something to look forward to tomorrow. We can have breakfast together.'

'Lovely. Goodnight.'

'Goodnight, Thea. Don't you think Justin could have said goodbye before he went home?'

Thea was seeing another side to Justin Anderson, a selfish one which she didn't like much. She ran down to her car and collected her luggage before returning to the pretty guest bedroom in Grace's apartment. Snapping on the light, she screamed.

'And exactly what are you doing in my bed?' she asked a sleepy Justin who merely rolled onto his back and looked up at her.

10

Thea would have done anything to have stopped Grace from being so upset the previous night. But what could she do when her bed had been taken over? Admittedly, there was no way Justin could have known Thea was staying with his sister. It was all a horrible misunderstanding and Justin had been unhappy to be sent home. The sooner Thea got on with trying to organise a workable programme about the Baker brothers and their horrendous activities, the sooner she could be away from the district. She liked Grace and hoped they'd be able to continue their friendship, but she wanted no involvement with Justin.

Dressed in cotton trousers and a light sweater, Thea left the bedroom and searched for Grace. She wasn't in the flat. Knowing she wouldn't mind, Thea put the kettle on for a cup of tea. Then she sat down with her pad and pen hoping to come up with ideas for the exposé. It was no use, every time she let her mind loose on the Baker brothers' behaviour all she saw were the poor creatures on Justin's land and the man himself. She wished she could forget about him. When Grace's phone rang, she hesitated before answering it.

'Is Justin there?'

'Rae? Is that you? It's Thea. Grace isn't here at the moment. I've no idea where she is.'

'Thea. How nice. Are you okay? What are you doing at Grace's?'

'She invited me to stay. But you asked about Justin. He's not here either, although he did come round yesterday evening.'

'He's vanished then,' said Rae. 'Not your problem. By the way, did you see his stupid behaviour in the press?' Thea remained silent, but Rae didn't appear to notice as she carried on, 'Of course, anyone would be a fool to believe what they saw. Except that Grace isn't a fool but she will have believed it. It was all carefully edited and distorted, I'm sure. I've seen it time and again. Ask Justin to call me or the studio if he turns up. Are you coming over to visit us? I'll let Milly know.'

As soon as they'd said goodbye, the front door opened. 'I'm so pleased you're back,' Thea said, beaming until she saw it wasn't Grace.

'You've changed your tune,' said Justin, standing tall and handsome in the doorway. 'Last night you couldn't wait to get rid of me. Come on, Thea, we must sort this out. I hate fighting with you.'

'Is Grace all right?'

'Of course she is. She's popped along the corridor to take some biscuits to her friend. I met her on my way up. She said you were still asleep.'

'Rae rang and says you've to get in touch with her or the studio immediately.' She headed for the bedroom, intent on getting away from Justin. She didn't want to hear his lame excuses. But what if Rae had been right and the news stories *had* been edited in a malicious way. People were always doing this to celebrities. She'd ask Justin what happened. As she turned to retrace her steps, she found her feet stepping on his shiny shoes.

'You've done it again.' He shook his head at her. 'At least they haven't left a mark this time.' His mouth curled and he laughed. Thea found it infectious and joined in, but was interrupted by her phone ringing. It was Hermione.

'I need you in London *now*, Thea.'

'I'm supposed to be working on the cruelty report, Dave said.'

'Well, Dave has been called away. There's some sort of financial difficulty which he's got to convince people is only temporary, so he's having a meeting with the backers. As you know, Thea, there are likely to be staff cuts. Just do what I say. If you don't prove yourself useful you'll be the first to go. You'll just have to be a bit imaginative about your report.'

Thea couldn't believe what she was hearing. Surely Dave wouldn't stand for sloppily sourced reporting. 'But I want it to be factually correct and I want to interview some of the locals. See what they've got to say about the Bakers.'

'It's hardly going to get much of an audience. I mean which would you rather watch? Mangy animals or Justin Anderson.'

Justin was looking at her quizzically.

'Okay, Hermione, I'll leave now. Bye.'

'What's wrong, Thea?' Justin asked.

'I've got to go back to work.'

'Stay and have lunch with me, please. Then you can tell me why I got the cold shoulder last night.'

'It doesn't matter. Let's be realistic. We live in different worlds. Yours is full of glamorous women and mine is full of . . . Hermione.'

Justin slumped on the sofa and barely acknowledged her when she hurriedly left the apartment.

She hung around by the lifts until

Grace appeared from one of the other doors on her floor. 'Thea, what's going on? You've got your luggage. It's not Justin again is it? He's not driving you away? After all that fuss last night and then him getting a taxi home I didn't think he'd show his face today.'

'No, it's not him. I've been called back to the office. I'm sorry. I loved staying with you.'

Grace reached out to hug her. 'Come again. And soon. I can't wait.'

⋆   ⋆   ⋆

Hermione was once again using Thea as the office junior. Thea endured three days of drudgery before Dave returned looking drawn and haggard.

'Thea! I thought you were off in the wilds doing that animal story.'

'I was called back.'

'Personal problems? Let's go into my office.'

Thea liked Dave as he seemed straightforward, but after the discussion about him and Hermione, she'd seen him in a different light. She tried not to dwell on the idea that Dave had cheated on the sweet-looking and attractive woman in the photo on his desk.

'So, Thea, what's all this about?'

'I had to come. I'm in a difficult position. When you're not around Hermione is in charge and she said I was needed here. I don't want to tell tales though.'

'That's what makes you different from her, your decency. Look I don't want this to get out, but Hermione won't be working here for much longer. I'm giving her the Justin Anderson story as her send-off.'

'But I assumed . . . ' Thea could feel herself flushing. She should really think *before* she opened her mouth.

'What did you think?' Dave fiddled with the pen on his desk. 'Come on, Thea, be honest.'

'I thought Hermione had some hold over you.'

Dave roared with laughter. 'You thought she was blackmailing me! You've certainly got a good imagination.'

'I'm going to need one if I can't get back and get some facts on the Bakers.' She hoped this would steer him away from the previous topic of conversation.

'You can't side-track me. What hold could Hermione possibly have over me?' He laughed again. 'Dear sweet Thea. You thought we'd had an affair and she'd threatened to tell my wife. You've been researching me, I suppose, and have found the stories speculating on me carrying on with Hermione, haven't you? Am I right?'

Thea nodded, wishing the floor would open and swallow her up.

Dave steepled his fingers and continued, 'I know I didn't deny it at the time, but nor did I confirm it. It seemed kinder that way. My wife understood and we both knew there would soon be bigger and better stories to take the public interest. Let me tell you about

Hermione. She met and fell in love with an actor, Ged Gibbings. You'll have seen him in older films although he's pretty much over the hill now. But he was only using her to get publicity. As soon as he'd got what he wanted he dropped her. She was broken-hearted. Difficult to imagine, isn't it? She's become bitter and brittle since then and although I've given her more chances than most employers would, it's not working out, not for me, the company or the other people who work here.'

Thea felt awful. 'I'm sorry I drew the wrong conclusion. In my heart I know you aren't the type of man to cheat on his wife.'

★　★　★

Thea was kept busy negotiating with Zach and Unwin's solicitor and trying to find local people who would give her balancing views of the brothers.

Despite what Hermione said, Thea would either report properly or not at all. She'd outlined her proposal to Dave and he'd given her the go-ahead with legal limitations. By immersing herself in the dubious world of the two criminals, she was able, in part, to distance herself from Justin. Her unconscious world, however, was not so easily controlled, and her dreams were filled with him. Sometimes she'd wake feeling happy only to realise that his arms around her were only a fantasy.

A phone call from Dave alerted Thea to the broadcast of Justin's story. 'Tune in tomorrow evening at seven thirty. Or you can come over here and watch if you prefer.'

Thea rubbed her forehead and acknowledged how tired she was. 'I'm quite busy,' she said, truthfully, 'so I'll probably watch at home. Thanks for letting me know, Dave. How are you?'

'Good, I'm good, thanks for asking. No one seems to do that these days.' He laughed down the telephone line. 'You still don't want to let me know what happened between you and Justin?'

'We found we weren't made for each other.'

'I won't pry. Let me know what you think of the insert, won't you?'

'If you've been overseeing it, I'm sure it'll be perfect,' said Thea.

★   ★   ★

Feeling anxious at seeing Justin, although not face to face, Thea sat in front of the television set with a large glass of wine and notebook and pen. She'd set the recorder and was determined to view Hermione's work with a producer's eye.

As soon as Justin appeared on the screen, Thea's heart jumped. He seemed to be looking straight at her and it was as if they were the only two people in the world. Then Hermione's voice cut in and Thea came back down to earth. A lot of the time, Thea mouthed the words as her own questions were asked. She was surprised that Hermione had included so much of her work.

'And these animals you have here, Justin, they belong to you, is that correct?'

'My sister and I are looking after them,' replied Justin, smiling at the camera.

'Looking after them? I don't think I would call it looking after them. Perhaps the viewers can decide.'

Thea's hand flew to her mouth as the camera panned the field where the wretched animals were. The sores on the horses' back and the ribs sticking through Milly's flesh were in close-up. Put the picture together with the commentary and anyone watching would be shocked. Gulping down some wine, Thea searched her mind frantically as to what she could do to stop this going pear-shaped. Then she conceded that it was too late. Horrified, she continued to watch the box in the corner of her room as it transmitted pictures and sounds from the pitiful creatures.

The phone rang and Rae seethed,

'What's going on? Can't you stop it?'

Thea struggled to find something to say, but couldn't. Rae gave up and cut the call. Not sure what to do, Thea rang Dave. 'I don't know what the hell's going on, Thea, get off the line while I see if I can stop it.'

Hermione was continuing, 'I think you're getting the picture of the real Justin Anderson. The one who doesn't care a lot about suffering. I hope you'll remember these deplorable pictures when you next think you'll go and watch Izaak Flanagan at the cinema.'

The camera homed in on Milly once more before a close-up of Justin who was smiling at his audience. 'Hermione's changed her wording after the filming with Justin,' gasped Thea. 'He's responding to my script.' Thea knew Justin would be watching. Despite their coolness to one another lately, she picked up the phone and waited for him to answer.

When the call went through to voicemail Thea felt like crying. She had to explain to Justin this wasn't what she'd intended when she'd planned the interview.

Thea spent the next few hours trying to get in touch with Justin and Dave, but their phones were busy or she went through to voicemail. Neither of them wanted to talk to her. She was startled when her phone rang. 'Justin?'

'No, Thea, it's Dave. All hell's broken loose. I've got Justin's lawyer on his way to see me now. Justin has already lost the contract for further Izaak Flanagan films. His career will be in ruins. I've got reporters trying to storm the building. But I wanted you to know none of this is your fault. It's all down to Hermione. She was taking her revenge on anyone who remotely resembled Ged Gibbings.'

'I don't get how it happened.'

'It's an old trick. I've seen it before and I should have been prepared. It's a neat way of wreaking vengeance. Hermione knew she was history and she couldn't just slink away, she had to create an uproar. We looked at the recorded insert together, made a couple of changes and agreed it was good. She must have convinced a couple of our production team to help her with the extra filming and re-edit. No doubt she told them it was on my say so. Why the commissioning channel broadcast it I have no idea. Hermione's made Justin appear callous and succeeded in wrecking his career. Hold on . . . I've got to go. Speak soon.'

Thea chewed at her nail. Her heart went out to Justin. His career would be over and all because of lies put out by a bitter and revengeful woman. She must talk to someone who would know how he was.

'Hi, Grace, Thea here, sorry if I've woken you. How's Justin?'

'I'm not sure. Toby's taken him to a secret location. He's received all sorts of threats, even death threats, from animal rights activists. It's so unfair. Lies, all lies.' Heart-wrenching sobs followed.

'I don't know what to say, Grace, I feel responsible.'

'We all know it's not your fault. If only . . . '

Yes, if only, Thea thought. There were so many if onlys. 'I'd like to talk to Justin, but I'm just getting his voice-mail.'

'He's not using his old number. Only Toby, Rae and I are allowed to know the new one. Sorry. It's just that he was getting so many hateful calls.'

'That's appalling. Will you be all right? And what about Rae? Where's she?'

'You know Rae, she's staying at the house. She can't leave the animals to fend for themselves. And I'll be fine. Toby's going to come here and stay once he's dropped Justin off. I'll speak to Justin and see if he'll give you a call.'

It was only in the early hours of the morning that Thea finally dropped off to sleep. She'd spent forever watching her phone hoping that it would spring into life and bring the man she loved back into her world.

A shower revived her slightly and she decided to head to the local café for some strong coffee and a sweet, sticky Danish. As she passed the newsagents she couldn't help but notice the headlines. They ranged from Sick Star Starves Animals to Izaak Flanagan Disgraced. Her appetite deserted her. Sitting in the café sipping her coffee, she wondered if there was any way to put this right. And there was. Just as soon as her programme about the Bakers was aired everyone would know that Justin was innocent. She quickly pressed Dave's number. 'It's me. I think I'd better get my exposé completed and broadcast as soon as possible. It might take the heat off Justin and that should calm things down for you too.'

'The sooner the better, Thea. You can use all the resources you want. If you can get it completed by this time next week I can negotiate a prime time slot.'

'No pressure then?'

'No pressure,' Dave chuckled.

'It's great to hear you laugh again.'

'I don't feel much like laughing, what with the financial difficulties and now this Hermione-created disaster. But I have a lot of faith in you. If anyone can put this right it's you.'

Thea knew that Justin's future was in her hands. If it meant working twenty-four hours a day she'd do it. This was the challenge of her life and she wasn't going to let herself or Justin down.

11

'Thea Stafford.' Thea automatically answered her phone as she was scribbling notes onto her pad. A soft voice was at the other end of the line and she had to strain to listen. 'Who's calling, please?' Then she got a bit anxious. What if it was some troublemaker who wanted to make more fuss for Justin? She raised her voice and inflected it with authority. 'What do you want?'

'Thea, it's me. Don't you recognise my voice?'

'No, I don't, and if you don't enlighten me I'm ending the conversation,' she said, wishing she'd screened the call.

'It's Toby.'

Thea squealed and then let out a long breath. 'Oh, Toby. You should have called me ma'am then I'd have known it was you.'

'You're Thea to me now.'

Silence hung between them until Thea said, 'How are you? And Justin?' Saying his name made her stomach lurch. She waited impatiently for the answer. What was going on? It was a straightforward question and it should have been an equally easy answer.

'I'm fine. Justin's . . . well, Justin's not good. I've just been to check on him.'

'Is he ill?' Thea was worried. Things were falling apart and, although she knew it wasn't her fault, she somehow felt responsible. 'Can I do anything?'

'He's trying to blot things out, I think. That's the only explanation I can come up with.'

'I'd like to see him, Toby.'

'Not possible, I'm afraid. He's not receptive to visitors at the moment.' Toby cleared his throat. 'I don't suppose I should say this, but he's drinking, Thea. I've never known him like this before.'

'He's worked so hard to get himself

up to the top; it must be tough for him.'

'It's more than that,' said Toby, flatly. 'I've got to go.'

'Can I get in touch?' But the line was dead and when Thea searched for the number Toby had called from, it had been withheld.

★   ★   ★

Muzzy from lack of proper sleep, and worry, Thea drove to the place which had been her home for a short time, the place where she'd been happy. Although she knew Justin was a public figure, she was overwhelmed by the news media camped out around his estate.

Hoping to recapture a little of the joy she'd known there, she was unprepared for the reception she got when she eventually found Rae at the horses' shelter.

'What do you want?' asked Rae, standing, hands on hips, looking furious. 'Come to make things worse, have you?'

'Rae, I . . . ' Thea was devastated. She had no right to be here, Justin didn't want to speak to her and Rae was hostile as well. It would be better to get on with interviewing the local people about Unwin and Zach and then get back to her little flat.

As she left, she risked a backward glance. Justin's sister was leaning against the fence sobbing her eyes out. Running back, Thea put her arms around Rae's thin shoulders and held her until she'd run out of tears.

'I'm sorry,' gulped Rae. 'But things are awful. Justin's a mess, the animals are going to suffer because I can't look after them on my own and if Justin doesn't have an income, the vet won't get paid and we'll have to sell this place and the animals won't have a home and Grace will have to move out of her lovely, but expensive, apartment and . . . and I feel sorry for myself.' Rae took a crumpled tissue from her pocket and blew her nose before giving Thea a slight smile.

★　★　★

Thea felt as though she'd been of some help to at least one member of Justin's family. She'd insisted on taking Rae back to the house and practically forced her to eat some soup and toast. Handing her a cup of tea she asked, 'Feeling a bit better?'

'It's good having you here to share my feelings. I was so angry with you when I was watching the programme, but I knew it couldn't be down to you. Remember how many times I've caught you and Justin snogging?'

Thea tried to put those thoughts from her mind and concentrate on making things easier for Rae. 'I know now that Justin's not interested in me romantically, but I would like to be of assistance to him, just as a friend.'

Rae nodded. 'He's shut himself off from us all.'

'Can I go and see him?'

'Are you some sort of masochist? He'll slam the door in your face.'

'I can deal with that. I feel responsible for this horrible mess, Rae, I need the opportunity to at least try and put it right.'

'Yeah, I know.'

⋆ ⋆ ⋆

Trembling as she rang the doorbell, Thea hoped that Justin would answer the door of the secluded cottage. At any other time she would have embraced the beauty of the area and taken time to enjoy the sea view. The cottage was in an idyllic position perched on the cliff top and the drive up the lane had been rough enough to put off the most intrepid reporter. But she hoped her old banger hadn't been damaged.

'Who is it?' Justin asked from behind the door.

'Me, Thea. I'd like to talk to you, try and explain.'

'Go home, Thea, get on with your job of ruining lives.'

She heard his footsteps echoing as he

moved away. She thumped on the door. 'Let me in! I'm not going anywhere until you let me talk to you, you stubborn man.' There was no response.

Making her way through the overgrown garden she headed round the back. The rose thorns scratched at her legs and arms, but nothing was going to stop her. Peering through the grubby kitchen window she could see Justin slumped at a large wooden table littered with empty bottles.

She tried the latch of the door, but it was bolted from inside. She banged again. 'Stop being so childish and let me in. It's so mean of you. Open the door,' she called again. There was a crash, then she heard bolts being scraped back and a key being turned. The door opened and the man standing before her didn't look like the Justin Anderson she'd fallen in love with. This one was bleary-eyed, unshaven and wearing crumpled, grubby clothes.

'Oh, Justin,' she cried, wrapping her arms around him.

He staggered backwards and bumped into the table. 'Get away from me,' he slurred, waving his arms around. 'Clear off and leave me alone.'

Thea wished she *had* stayed away. She hated seeing Justin like this. 'Please,' she implored, 'don't get rid of me. Let me explain.'

'I'm not interested. I don't want to hear.' Justin put his hands over his ears and cowered from her. 'You're seriously bad news, you know that?'

'I know,' said Thea. 'I came to apologise and to explain, but you don't want to know, do you?'

Justin shook his head. 'I want my life back.'

Studying him objectively for a split second, Thea saw a pathetic figure. Was she wasting her time on him? she wondered.

Then Justin seemed to make a mammoth effort to pull himself together. 'I've nothing to say to you.'

'That's because you're drunk,' said Thea.

'I am. I have been since I got here,' Justin gave her a lopsided grin.

'Then you should be ashamed of yourself,' lectured Thea, hoping to shame him into sobering up.

'Leave me alone. Please.' Justin slumped down into a chair, lifted a whisky bottle to his mouth, hesitated and put it back on the table. 'Please go away. I hate you to see me like this.'

Thea's instinct was to go to him and hold him, but something told her to back off. She went through a doorway at the far end of the kitchen which brought her to an untidy sitting room. Plonking herself on the sofa, she put her feet up, absently watching the television which was already switched on. Although she could understand his reaction, part of Thea wanted to shake Justin until he sobered up and tried to salvage what remained of his career. Even though he'd done nothing wrong, he'd have to earn forgiveness from his formerly adoring fans who must have felt let down by him, but he could do it, she was sure. And there was the bonus, she hoped, of her programme about the Baker brothers which would surely exonerate him. Feeling she might be wasting time with Justin, she dithered as to whether it would be more useful to stay at the cottage or leave to get on with her project. Her notebook was never far away and, deciding to hone the notes she'd made, Thea brought it out. As she did so, something on the television caught her interest.

'Justin! Justin!' she called, sitting upright and paying attention.

He staggered into the room and threw himself down on the sofa next to her. 'What d'you want?'

'Look at the news.' She grabbed his hand, held it tightly and watched as Justin tried to focus on the scene being shown.

'That's a fire,' he said before closing his eyes.

'Oh, Justin, it's at your place. Look, there's the barn. We've got to get back. What about Rae? This is terrible.'

'Leave me alone, let me sleep.'

Thea rushed into the kitchen and made some very strong coffee. Back in the sitting room she found Justin snoring loudly with his mouth hanging open. 'Wake up! Wake up!' Having slapped him awake she made him drink the coffee. 'Now, we're going in my car.'

'I'll drive,' he slurred.

'No, *I'll* drive and you'll sleep.' Her hands were trembling and she felt sick with worry. Rae wasn't answering her phone.

Driving back gave her too much time to think and consider all the possible consequences of the fire. She didn't know how Justin and Grace would cope with anything happening to Rae. She glanced at her passenger, who now seemed to be sleeping peacefully, totally unaware of what they were about to face.

12

As they neared Justin's estate, Thea had to pull off the road as a fire engine, siren blaring and lights flashing, tore past.

'What's that?' Justin asked.

Turning off the engine she took his hand again. 'Justin, do you know where we're going?'

'Home. You're taking me home.'

'We're going home because there's been a fire. It was on the news.'

Justin frowned, then suddenly sobered up as he understood. 'Rae's there. Is the house on fire? We've got to get there.'

They could see flames and smoke above the tree tops as they made their way up the drive. When Thea came to a halt, she was relieved to see that the house was still intact and hopefully Rae was safe. There were several fire engines working on the blazing barn.

Putting her arm round Justin, she led him over to one of the firemen who was taking a rest, his face blackened by the dense smoke.

'This is the owner of the property, Justin Anderson. Is his sister safe?'

'You mean the feisty young woman, Rae? She insisted on being with the animals as they'd be scared by all the noise. I'm sorry, sir, but everything in the barn will be destroyed.'

'That's all right. Rae's safe. That's what matters. Come on, Thea.' He grabbed her hand and was about to lead her off to the shelters when Thea's investigative instinct kicked in. 'How did the fire start? Do you know?'

'Not yet, there'll be an enquiry. But it's almost certainly arson.'

'The Bakers. I'll kill them.' Justin let go of Thea's hand and was about to head off down the drive.

'No, Justin, don't. Rae needs you now. Let's find her.'

As Thea and Justin rounded the field, they saw her crooning to the animals, just as she had so many times before. When she saw them, Rae waved and beckoned them over. 'At least they're all right. A bit scared, but not physically harmed. How could the Baker brothers have done it? Aren't they in police custody or something, out of harm's way?'

'It wasn't them.' Toby stood a little way off, surveying the smoking barn in the distance.

'Come off it, Toby, who else would want to inflict this on Justin and Rae?' asked Thea. 'It has to be the work of Zach and his brother.'

Toby shook his head. 'I saw the news on the television. When I visited Justin I thought I should go to the town to get provisions and Justin seemed, well, he was resting. There's a very good steak house there . . . ' He hesitated, glancing sideways at Rae. 'Sorry,' he said. 'Anyway, the news was on and I saw the devastation here and came straightaway. I had a strange feeling, can't explain it. It didn't seem to be the work of Zach and Unwin. I got here soon after the fire started and found this.' He handed a piece of paper to Justin who grabbed it.

'Animal rights? But why would they target us? We take the animals in, look after them, give them a good home.' He shook his head as if to make sense of things.

'You do,' agreed Toby, 'but if anyone had been watching that awful bit on you it's obvious how it might have looked, isn't it?'

Rae caught on quickly. 'That's why they've targeted the barn. Justin's cars are in there. Thank goodness they didn't want to hurt the animals.'

'I'm sure we've got a lot to be thankful for,' said Toby, grimly, 'but at the moment, I can't think of much.'

'Grace,' yelled Rae. 'What will she be thinking?'

'I'll ring her,' offered Thea, wanting to be useful.

'It's okay, I've put her in the picture,' sighed Toby. 'Justin, I think you'd be better out of here. You're still hot news with the media. You'll be hounded.'

'I'm not leaving Rae on her own,' declared Justin moving to his sister's side and putting a protective arm around her.

'Oh get off, I'm capable of looking after myself. You smell awful. I think Toby's right, you should go.'

Backing off, Justin looked sheepish. 'I've been really stupid and irresponsible, haven't I? Sorry everyone.'

'I'm sorry about your cars,' said Rae. 'Pity the police didn't hang on to your green sports car a bit longer, then it might have been saved.'

Justin shrugged. 'I'll get over it. Hey, what is it, Thea?'

'I really wanted to drive that red car of yours,' she said, pleased to lighten the atmosphere a little.

'I'll buy you one, then, if it means that much to you,' promised Justin.

'It's all I stuck around for,' smiled Thea. Her brain was working furiously wondering how she could angle a story about the animal rights activists. Their hearts were probably in the right place, but their actions were reckless. What would have happened if a cat or a dog, or even a human, had been sheltering in the barn? Or if the fire had spread in the direction of the horses? She went over to stroke the donkey. 'Hi, Milly, remember me?' Without warning, the donkey turned its back and kicked up its hind legs missing Thea by a hair's breadth. 'I see you do.'

★   ★   ★

Thea waited a couple of days before phoning Justin to check how things were.

'I'm fine, no thanks to you,' he said angrily.

'But . . . '

'My sister might have been killed in the fire and all because I let you stay with us and get close. You got to know more about our lives than anyone outside family and friends ever has before. My mistake.'

'But on the night of the fire you were fine with me. You joked that you'd buy me a car. I thought we might be all right again.'

'You were mistaken. Maybe I gave you the wrong message, but I was relieved Rae and the animals were safe and I was still fuzzy from my drinking binge. My emotions were all over the place. Thank you for getting me back to the house, but there would have been no fire if it hadn't been for you.'

⋆ ⋆ ⋆

Thea couldn't bear to watch her programme with anyone else so was sitting at home alone, tensely waiting for it to begin. She'd rung Rae and told her when it was on and suggested she let the others know. She'd had no word from Justin since his harangue. She understood how protective he was of his family and realised that he didn't want his fame or infamy to impact on them. But she had been very unhappy that he'd blamed her for something which had been totally out of her control.

He'd become the subject of massive media controversy, trending on twitter and all over Facebook. Some people thought Justin deserved to lose his collection of rare and vintage cars, and some thought he should lose much more. Her stomach was in knots. What if the broadcast didn't save Justin's career and reputation? She screwed her eyes shut when the introductory music started, then forced herself to watch. It was too late now. There was nothing more she could do.

*　*　*

Since the show had ended, her phone hadn't stopped ringing and texts kept buzzing in. Thea ignored them. All she wanted to do was curl up in bed and stay there for a very long time. It had come across exactly as she'd hoped and planned, but now she had to wait for the next day's papers to see if Justin had been cleared of any wrongdoing by the jury of the media and public. She didn't have the heart to check social media, some of the stuff on there was so vicious and personal.

In spite of her exhaustion she spent the night tossing and turning and, after finally falling into a deep sleep, was woken by a pounding on the door. Throwing on jeans and a t-shirt, she pulled the door open to find Dave beaming at her through a forest of flowers and foliage. 'For you,' he said, thrusting the bouquet into her arms.

Thea inhaled their scent, 'They're beautiful, my favourite, roses. Come in, I'll put the kettle on.'

'No, you sit down and rest. I'll bung these in the sink and you can find a vase later. You look dreadful.'

'Thanks.' Thea did as she was told and waited as Dave produced toast and coffee.

'So, what's the verdict?' she asked

when he'd sat down.

'Brilliant, it was one of the best things we've come up with in a long time.'

'Good.' She could hardly bring herself to ask the question again. 'I meant, what's the verdict on Justin?'

'I don't believe you, Thea. Haven't you seen or heard any news at all this morning? Aren't you on twitter?'

'I was asleep. You woke me.'

Dave jumped up and switched on the TV then flicked to a twenty-four hour news channel. 'Watch this for a bit. I've got to go, but take the rest of the week off. We'll see you Monday.'

'There's nothing about Justin,' Thea said, disappointed.

'There's another big story. Politicians wasting taxpayers' money. But the second main story is Justin and it's good news, Thea, very good news.'

Thea could feel tears welling in her eyes. 'Sorry, Dave, it's such a relief.'

Dave sat down again. 'You do know that Justin isn't anything like Ged

Gibbings. From what I know, Justin is a decent bloke. He's not the sort to use someone for his own ends like Ged did.'

Thea sniffed, 'I know.'

'On the subject of Ged, I think you ought to know the whole story about Hermione and why she did what she did. It's not an excuse, just an explanation. There was an interview with Ged, just after his marriage to Cate Planter. You know, she recently won an Oscar as supporting actress in 'Distraction Comes Easily'. He was asked about Hermione. Had he had an affair with her et cetera? He said Cate was the only woman he'd ever loved and that he hardly knew Hermione. She meant nothing to him. Total lies, of course. We all know they were together for years, just until he'd got the publicity he wanted. He went on to be quite nasty about her. All I can say is that it tipped her over the edge. I suppose she saw Justin as a younger version of Ged and decided to get her revenge. Not a rational move, but Hermione hasn't always been rational. Hey, look, they're showing the front pages of the newspapers. I'll let myself out.'

Thea couldn't tear her eyes from the screen. The headline ran 'Izaak Flanagan Returns' and the newsreader was smiling as she said, 'Justin Anderson is the people's hero as the truth behind the outrageous profile presented by Hermione Clutterbuck unfolded in a spectacular way yesterday. Dave Clarkson of FPC said it was down to one person, Thea Stafford. She alone was responsible for exonerating Justin Anderson. Dave added that he had never known two more likeable and caring people than Thea and Justin and he had known all along that Justin could never have done the things of which he was accused.'

It was all over. Thea gave herself up to the emotions which had threatened to overwhelm her ever since she'd first met Justin Anderson. Finally she fell asleep on the sofa and when she woke up it was late afternoon. The television was still switched on and there was Justin smiling at her, saying that he was grateful for all the people who had stood by him and believed in him.

After he'd disappeared from the screen, Thea switched off the television and gave her attention to texts and voicemail. The two she was most interested in were from Justin and Hermione. Eager to hear Justin's voice, she listened.

'Hi, Thea,' his intimate tone came along the line. 'I wanted to say a big thank you for helping me out with this situation. I owe you and I'd like to see you. Please call me when you're free. And I'm very sorry for the other day now that I know the truth about what happened.'

At any other time Thea would have called instantly, but she was intrigued as to what Hermione had to say. Besides, Justin had judged her rather harshly and she was still feeling raw from his anger and lack of trust. 'Thea, we need to talk. Meeting at the office isn't a good idea. I'll be in the coffee shop on Parade Walk at seven this evening.'

The woman doesn't change, does she? thought Thea. Still as bossy as ever.

As she dialled Justin's mobile number, her tummy tensed. Everything was going to be all right. Or was it? A frown creased her forehead as she waited. There was no reply. The phone flipped to voicemail and Thea left a curt message to say she was returning his call. If he'd really wanted to be in touch with her he'd have answered his phone, wouldn't he?

Scrolling through her messages, she listened and deleted most of them, having noted the callers. Once again, Hermione's voice reverberated through her and she held the phone away from her ear. Listening to the tone, Thea caught the pathos and hesitated. Then she shook her head and told herself not to be so soft. There was no way she would meet up with Hermione. But after having a shower and putting on some fresh clothes, she changed her mind.

★ ★ ★

Thea had time for a quick snack before setting off. She was tucking into cheese on toast when the doorbell rang. To her amazement and muted joy, Justin was at the door. She didn't invite him in.

'May I come in?'

'I don't think so. I'm about to go out.'

'Please, Thea. I know I've been unreasonable. It's just that the media have hounded me from day one. I don't know who to trust. I felt I'd been stitched up by you and FPC.'

Her stomach was doing somersaults. He was looking fantastic and his complexion no longer had the sickly pallor she'd seen at the cottage. Although she was feeling a bit ambivalent towards him at the moment, she had to admit that he exuded healthy energy as he stood on her doorstep obviously anxious to step inside. Thea relented a little and opened the door to let him in.

'I know I've been an idiot and very unkind. I'm sorry. I can't say it enough. I'm asking you to forgive me. Please, Thea,' he begged.

Thea thought she understood why he'd been so harsh with her, but his accusations had hurt her badly.

Justin reached for her hand and held it to his lips. She didn't pull away. 'What I'd like more than anything is for you and me to go to a desert island and spend time getting to know each other properly without all the media attention and, much as I love them, without my sisters. I've been getting nothing but grief from them recently.'

Thea giggled. She could just imagine Rae and Grace giving Justin a tough time. Not that he didn't deserve it. Then she became serious as Justin reached out and stroked her hair. 'I've been a fool.'

'I agree.'

As they moved closer Justin tilted her chin.

She pulled away. 'I don't think I'm ready for this. How *are* Rae and Grace?'

'They're great. I'm relieved things can stay as they are. Grace happily living in her flat and Rae looking after her animals.'

'I haven't seen anything about a police investigation into the fire. Have they caught the culprits?'

'They're getting there. Rae did a bit of delving. She got some useful information from some of her contacts. The people who set fire to the barn are a breakaway faction from a legitimate group campaigning against laboratory testing. Rae's getting involved. You know Rae!'

Thea smiled. 'I don't know how these people so misjudged you. It's so obvious you're the sort of person who'd be kind to any living thing.'

'Don't you remember when you first came to the house? *You* misjudged me too. You thought I was being cruel and stormed off, remember?'

'I was upset. I didn't want to believe you were cruel, but the evidence was there in front of me.'

'Exactly. We all make mistakes, incorrect assumptions about people. I was mistaken about you. I should have trusted you.'

When he reached out for her this time she relaxed into his arms and their lips met. It felt so right to be with him, so she gave herself up to her emotions and lost herself in him.

Then, abruptly she pulled away. 'I've got an appointment.'

'Can't you cancel it? I'd like to take you out. Somewhere special.'

'That's not possible. I've agreed to meet Hermione.'

Justin's expression changed to one of disappointment. 'You're meeting Hermione even after she nearly ruined my career. Okay, I'll be in touch later.'

13

Thea spotted Hermione in the café on Parade Walk and took a few moments to study her without being observed. She looked older and very tired. Poor woman can't have had a happy life, thought Thea. Then a nagging voice insisted that if Hermione was more sensitive to other people perhaps she'd have more friends. About to open the door, Thea drew in a startled breath as she watched Hermione take from her bag what looked like a cardboard box of tablets, extracting a couple and swallowing them. If she'd harboured any thoughts of sloping off and ignoring Hermione, there was no way she could now.

'Hermione, how are you?' asked Thea, not sure how to act now she was in close proximity to her former colleague.

'Thea. Thank you for coming. Let me get you a coffee.' Hermione looked around and for one horrible moment Thea thought she was going to snap her fingers at the waitress. But Hermione was smiling and Thea was instantly on her guard.

Sitting with their drinks, the two women stared at each other. 'I won't be coming back to work, Thea. Dave said he can't afford me which I understand as I command top salary these days.' Her eyes narrowed, 'I suppose you'll be trained to take over from me, but of course that will be well into the future.'

Thea felt her cheeks heating and squirmed in her chair. 'I've no idea what will happen next,' she said, truthfully.

'Justin Anderson is only an actor, don't trust him. He'll lead you along, seduce you with his looks and his money and then leave you stranded while he trades you in. You saw what happened in Sweden, it won't be a one-off, believe me!'

'Hermione, that has nothing to do with you.' Thea couldn't believe she'd been so silly as to have come here. What had she been hoping for? Some sort of reconciliation where Hermione admitted she'd been a fool and begged Thea's forgiveness for the way she'd behaved.

Hermione's hand crept across the table and grabbed claw-like at Thea's. 'I'm only giving you kindly advice,' she smiled. 'I know about actors.'

Thea tried to shake herself free from the older woman. 'Yes, I've heard what happened between you and Ged Gibbings and I'm truly sorry, Hermione, but that's in the past. Why not lighten up and look forward now?'

Abruptly Hermione loosened her grip and started to button her jacket. 'I won't say I told you so, but remember that I did.' She got up unsteadily and reached for her bag.

Watching Hermione stumble towards the door, Thea's inclination to let the woman go waned. Even though no thought had been given to make sure *she* had got home safely after the bicycle accident, it didn't seem right to simply hail a taxi and send her off. 'We can share a ride,' Thea said, even though she lived only a short distance away and had walked to the coffee shop in minutes. Although Thea didn't know Hermione's address, there was still no way she could let her travel on her own in this state. *And then what?* a little voice whispered. *You're going to act as a babysitter all evening?*

By the time they arrived at Hermione's rather classy house in the suburbs, her ex-colleague had perked up and was beginning to be her old spiky self. 'Don't imagine I'm going to pay for the taxi ride, Thea. As you know, I'm out of work!' She marched up the short drive, unlocked the front door and banged it shut leaving Thea open-mouthed.

To the amazement of the cab driver, Thea burst out laughing. At least she didn't have to feel sorry for Hermione anymore, she really was unbelievably awful.

★   ★   ★

As Dave had given her some time off, Thea decided to catch up with friends and she had Rae at the top of her list.

'Thea! How lovely to hear from you. I've been meaning to get in touch, but there's always so much to do. Please come and see me.'

'I'd love to Rae, but . . . '

'I know, that stupid brother of mine. He's not here and he won't be back for a few days. He's gone somewhere. After everything that's happened he said he needed to get away and have some time on his own to think things through.'

'In that case I'll come over today.'

'I've got so much to tell you. I've joined another group and we've got a meeting on Saturday.'

Thea grinned. Nothing stopped Rae, not the Baker brothers or the fire. She was one of life's survivors. Thea tried to put Justin from her mind and instead think how lucky it was that by working with him she'd met two lovely women who she hoped she'd stay friends with. But on the drive to see Rae, she couldn't help dwelling on the times she'd been with Justin. She was trying to be sensible, but couldn't deny that she'd fallen head over heels in love with him — just like thousands of other women. Realistically, he could pick and choose, and there was no reason for him to pick her when there were all those glamorous, sexy women in his celebrity world. Hermione was probably right.

Rae was in the kitchen cooking pasta and sauce when Thea arrived. 'You're just in time to do the salad. All the stuff's in the fridge.'

Thea was happy to help and listen to Rae chatting. But she knew that for her own peace of mind she'd have to bring up the subject of Justin.

'Justin's okay, then?'

'Yeah, I think so. Sort of. He was in a bit of a state, wasn't he, when everything kicked off after that horrible woman did the dirty on him? Then there was the fire, and he told me that you were friends with that awful woman and you chose to see her rather than go out with him. He was terribly hurt. I think he felt betrayed.'

'I'm not her friend and never will be. She asked to see me and I was intrigued to hear what she had to say. Justin turned up out of the blue. He couldn't expect me to just drop my plans.'

'I agree. He's completely trashed his relationship with you. I suppose I shouldn't tell you this, but before he went away he said that he'd fallen in love with you, but that you are far too good for him and there was no way you'd want to be with him and you deserved someone better.' Rae took a deep breath. 'He said he'd never met anyone like you before and that he didn't know how he'd live without you.'

'He said all that?'

'And more. But I think it was all meant to be confidential. I don't care, it's time you two got sorted out and if I can help then I will. Now tell me how you feel about him.'

'Well,' Thea resolutely chopped cucumber and peppers, 'I'm in love with him. It's as simple and as complicated as that.'

Rae shrugged. 'You two are hopeless.'

After eating, Rae insisted that Thea accompany her to the field, not that she needed much persuading.

Thea shivered as they passed the remains of the barn where the burnt-out vehicles were still visible. She was relieved to see diggers working and hoped a more secure garage would be erected soon.

'Hi, Milly,' she called over to the donkey, who was facing the other way. 'They're looking good, Rae. You give them so much care. I'm glad you've been awarded custody of the pigs. Goodness, they're growing really fat.' Thea bent to rub her fingers along a pink snout, getting a grunt in return. 'Tell me more about this meeting you're going to.'

'It's through the animal rights people,'

said Rae. 'Now don't look like that, Veronica's checked them out and they're legit. It was only that weird faction who was trouble. You can come with us if you like.'

'No thanks,' replied Thea immediately, not wanting to get involved. 'Let me know how you get on, though.'

The roar of a car engine made them both look at each other with raised eyebrows. 'Just in case,' said Rae, picking up the hefty branch of a tree.

'Whatever next?' muttered Thea.

The two women raced to the drive as the vehicle squealed to a halt.

'Justin? What do you think you're doing?' enquired Rae, still grasping the piece of wood. 'You told me you were going away.' She turned to Thea and said, 'Honestly, I had no idea. You'll think Grace and I lure you over to us, only to have our dear brother turn up. It's not like that at all.'

Thea knew that neither of the sisters would pull a trick like that, especially on her. She opened her mouth to reassure Rae, but Justin got in first, 'Are you following me, Thea? It seems I only have to be out of your sight for a short time before you're hounding me. I'll get the papers onto you.' He leaped out of the vehicle and loped towards her. As if magnetised, the two clung together as they smothered each other in kisses.

Rae put her hand to her mouth. 'Time I was going before I throw up.' She gave Thea a quick hug and said to Justin, 'Try and treat her well or she'll give up on you.'

'Will you?' asked Justin, releasing Thea a little and looking enquiringly at her.

Knowing the answer was 'never', Thea kept that to herself and played for time. 'There are a few things we've got to get sorted out, Justin. We need a long talk.'

He sighed. 'I know that. I came to see you to try and do exactly that, but you sent me away.'

'Only because I had an appointment . . . ' Thea began. 'This is no good, we're going round in circles. Rae said you'd gone away to think things over.' She didn't add that she knew the other titbits Rae had told her. Instead, she settled on, 'Did those things include me?'

'I found that I focused quite clearly once I asked myself what I wanted and what I would miss most,' said Justin, pulling her to him again.

'So you bought a new car?' said Thea, looking at the sleek red sports car. 'That looks familiar. How did you find exactly the same one?' Intrigued, Thea unravelled herself from Justin's embrace and walked around the car. When she saw the number plate, she froze.

'Thought you'd be surprised. That was the one you wanted to drive, wasn't it? I bought you exactly the same model,' said Justin. 'Will it do?'

Thea mouthed THEA ONE over and over.

'You do understand what it says, don't you?' Justin wanted to know.

'I think so,' whispered Thea.

'In case there's any doubt, it means that Thea is the one for me. There wasn't enough room for all of it.'

Thea laughed and cried at the same time. So what Rae had said was true, he did love her. How could she ever have doubted it?

'I expect you'll want to give it a go, won't you?' said Justin.

'I'm sure it'll work out, Justin. We love each other and that's a good starting point, don't you think?'

'The car,' he said, softly, dangling the keys in front of her hot face.

Thea snatched the keys from his hand. 'Come on then, let's go.' She jumped into the red TVR and started the engine and soon they were cruising down the country lanes both singing along with the radio at the top of their voices.

14

As Thea climbed the stairs to the office at FPC, she reflected on her time with Justin and his sisters. What a terrible time that family had faced, almost like a curse. Although Thea knew that Grace was not blood family, there was absolutely no doubt that she, Justin and Rae could not have been any closer. Thea wondered who the father of Grace's son was. Stop it, she told herself, sternly. It's nothing to do with you and it won't help anything.

'Thea, good to have you back on board,' beamed Dave as she bounded into the room. 'You can choose where you work. Would you like to change desks?'

'I'm happy with the one I had before,' said Thea, settling into the familiar chair; there was no way she wanted to move to the bigger desk by the window which had been Hermi-one's.

'We need more staff in this depart-ment now that we've come through our crisis in one piece,' continued Dave. 'Business is good, better than ever. We'll need to recruit at least two more office staff. You'll need a gofer, won't you?'

'Will I? Aren't *I* the gofer?' Thea was puzzled.

Dave wagged a finger at her. '*You* are a producer, Thea Stafford. You might have been a gofer in an earlier office life, but now you're assistant producer. We'll look at the contract later.'

'Oh, Dave, you're the greatest,' cried Thea leaping up to hug him enthusias-tically. 'I'll do my best to earn it, honestly I will.'

'You've already done a fair bit,' Dave assured her. He patted her back and said, 'Now, come on, let's get cracking.'

Thea sat back down and started sifting through the accumulated piles of papers. A beeping alerted Thea to an incoming text from Justin. Grinning inanely, Thea placed the phone on her desk and continued with the paper sorting, all the while feeling happy she would be seeing him in a couple of hours.

'Breaking news,' called Dave, yanking open his door. 'Someone's got to cover this, guess who?'

Thea looked round the otherwise empty room. 'Me?' she grinned. 'What's the story, Dave?'

'Some politician's disgraced himself, surprise, surprise. Better get down there and see if it will fit something I'm planning on the secret lives of people in power.'

Grabbing her phone, notebook and bag, she dashed from the room, only to retreat shamefacedly. 'Where did you say it was?'

'Get a cab to Parliament Square then follow your nose. All the media will be there, just barge your way through. I'll get a cameraman over asap.'

In the taxi, Thea made a call to Justin to explain why she wouldn't be able to make their date.'

'Okay then, newshound,' he said, 'I'll meet you somewhere else. Where are you going?'

'Parliament,' Thea told him.

'Very grand. I'll find you there.'

'But, Justin, I'm working and it'll be really crowded.'

'I can do crowds, remember?'

'But look what happened at the garden centre. It was awful.'

'I told you at the time that it comes with the territory. I can handle it. Don't worry, Thea, as I said, I'll find you.'

She smiled, put her phone in her bag and got her notebook ready. When she arrived at Parliament Square she found a sea of cameras and bodies. At first, she was polite, but it got her nowhere, so she did as Dave had advised and barged. The person who was being harangued by the press stood calm and tall, surrounded by security. He answered the questions adroitly and gave nothing away.

'Who is he?' asked Thea of the man standing next to her. He didn't answer and continued scribbling away. Thea decided to make notes and find out the politician's identity later.

As he was ushered away, Thea gave a satisfied sigh. She'd got the facts, but she did spare a thought for the man's wife and family who would be devastated by the story of his illegitimate children. She crammed her notebook in her bag and looked round for Justin. There was no sign of him so she pushed and shoved her way out of the crowd. The cameraman had done his stuff and was already making his way back to the office.

'Hey, Thea! Over here!'

She rushed over and gave Justin a hug. 'What's up? You look unhappy.'

'I'll explain over coffee.' He held her hand and led her to a snack bar where they ordered drinks.

'So what's happened now? Is it Rae?'

'No, it's Grace. One of the children they're talking about is her son.'

'You mean . . . he's the father?' Thea was shocked.

'Yes. Somebody, somehow, has found out he's the dad of several children with different women. Grace doesn't need this on top of everything else.'

'But no one has mentioned Grace. Surely if anyone knew Grace was the boy's mum it would have come out just now. There were all sorts of questions, but no one mentioned Justin Anderson's sister.'

'You know what? I don't care what it costs me, there are more important things in life than fame and fortune. But I do care what it might do to Grace.'

'That's why I love you.'

'It's all down to you. When all that business blew up about me being unkind to animals it tore me apart. It was so unjust. But now I realise the only things that really matter are my loved ones.'

'And the animals,' Thea said, taking his hand.

'Agreed.'

'Dave is going to be disappointed.'

'Why?'

'I'm not going to have anything to do with the story. I'd better go and tell him. He'll probably fire me.'

'And I'm going to see Grace. I'll suggest Toby takes her to the cottage I stayed at. They should be able to hide away there until this blows over. Let's hope she's strong enough to deal with it. I'll text or call you.'

As they kissed goodbye, Thea heard someone saying, 'Look, that's Justin Anderson. Let's get a selfie with him.'

★　★　★

Thea's heart hammered in her chest as she knocked on Dave's office door.

'Enter!'

'Dave, look, I'm sorry about this, but — '

'Please sit down Thea, I can't bear watching you hop from foot to foot. I'm sure whatever you're about to tell me can't be so bad.'

Thea sat in the chair opposite Dave and tried again. 'I can't do the story.'

'You mean the productive politician story? Why not?'

'I can't really tell you, but it's going to impact on people I love. I can't stop someone else doing the story, but I want no part of it.'

'Good, good.'

'What?'

'Believe it or not I like loyalty and integrity. But there's something that will suit you better. I've just been given some information about environmental damage being caused by one of the biggest companies in the UK. I've emailed the info as an attachment. I think it might interest you. I'm relying on you to come up with something big.'

Thea got a coffee from the machine and slumped at her desk hardly able to believe what she'd just heard. Dave was one in a million. So was Justin. She didn't deserve to be surrounded by such wonderful, loving, compassionate people.

Having opened the attachment, she started reading. The company mentioned had often been in the news because of its polluting production methods. They were definitely selfish and greedy, with no consideration for the environment.

Thea sought a new angle, one which would make people sit up and pay attention. She'd achieved it with the story about the Baker brothers and she was determined to give this story her best shot.

'Home time, Thea,' called Dave, coming out of his office. 'You don't live here, you know.'

Thea stretched and yawned. 'I need to finish this.'

Dave advanced to her desk. 'No, you need to go home. Work and rest in equal quantities is best. I should know, I've been trying to take my own advice for long enough.'

* * *

Thea microwaved a fish pie and took it onto her small balcony so she could enjoy the sunny evening. Then she remembered that Justin had said he'd be in touch. Food forgotten, she dashed to check her phone. There was a text and a voicemail. They informed her that Grace and Toby were at the secluded cottage, and that Grace was coping well. Justin added that he would be calling on Thea at half seven.

She saw she had about five minutes to get ready. Why hadn't she checked her phone before?

It had to be the quickest shower and change ever, but her reflection in the bedroom mirror showed she looked fresh enough to receive Justin. There was a rapping on the front door and when Thea opened it, she fell into Justin's arms.

'What a nice welcome,' he said, gently moving her backwards so he could shut the door behind him. 'You got my messages, then?'

'Only a few minutes ago,' confessed

Thea. 'I didn't leave work until late, I was busy.' She looked up at Justin's face and saw a frown crease his forehead. 'Not the politician story. Don't worry, Justin, I told Dave I couldn't do it. This is a new one. I'll tell you about it if you like.' One look at his face told her he wasn't in the least bit interested. In fact, all he seemed to be interested in was her. A fact which made her very happy indeed.

Later, the two of them sat on the sofa drinking coffee. 'Will you visit Grace?' Thea asked.

Justin shook his head. 'No, she knows I'm always here for her, but she has to work things out for herself. Does that sound harsh?'

Thea thought for a while. 'I'm not sure,' she admitted. 'I think you mean that problems will occur in her life and she shouldn't be reliant on you. After all, she has Toby.'

'Yes,' answered Justin, 'but more importantly, she must develop the confidence to live her life as she chooses. Taking the consequences of our actions and stuff, I suppose I mean.'

'I understand completely.'

'I've been pretty indulgent with Rae and all the things she's been involved with. I can't say I don't worry at times, but she has to learn for herself too.'

'You *are* generous when it comes to the animals.'

'I don't always feel like helping out or being tied down because Rae has gone off somewhere. I'm not especially happy about her getting involved in this activist group. I know most of them are okay. It's people like the ones who set fire to the barn that I worry about.'

'I expect Rae is a pretty good judge of character.'

'She is, she likes you.' He kissed her cheek. 'Anyway, I've made a decision about the animal refuge. I'll help at times, but I'm willing to pay for someone to work for Rae. Maybe that friend of hers, Veronica, would like the job, it's up to Rae to sort it out. I'm stepping back a bit from my sisters as I want to concentrate on other things.'

'Like your films? That's good.'

'No, not films, nothing like that. I've decided it's time to concentrate on you.'

'Me?'

'Yes, I want to know everything about you. I don't even know if you like surprises and then I went and surprised you with that car.' He put his arms round her. 'So tell me, do you like surprises?'

'I love them, but I can live perfectly happily without them.'

'And which city do you think is the most romantic in the world?'

'Definitely Paris.'

'And your favourite colour?'

'Blue.'

'I'll change the car then,' he teased.

'Don't you dare!'

'Favourite gem?'

'Pass, I don't have one.' She snuggled against him.

'I thought all women like diamonds.'

'I just don't have a favourite. I like all gems.'

'Favourite film character?'

'Izaak Flanagan.'

'Favourite actor?'

'Now what's that man's name? He was the detective in . . . '

'You have to tell the truth, Thea.'

'All right, I suppose it's you. Now, have I passed because if so I think we ought to carry on where we left off before coffee.'

Justin appeared to know the exact place they should carry on from and the two were soon entwined.

⋆ ⋆ ⋆

After their evening of passion Thea had hoped she would see more of Justin, but with the amount of work she had to do she had little time for anything, let alone dating. They spoke briefly on the phone and sent texts, but there were no more intimate evenings. She started to wonder if things would ever work out for them.

'Thea!'

'Justin, what are you doing at the office?'

'I've brought a surprise. For you!' From behind his back he produced a bunch of wild-looking blue flowers. 'I picked them from our gardens. Look closely.'

In amongst the greenery and petals Thea spotted a little blue box tied with delicate ribbon. As though Justin could read her mind he said, 'It's okay, I'm not making any presumptions. I wouldn't dare. It's just a gift.'

Lifting the lid, Thea found a delicate silver ring set with several sapphires. 'It's beautiful, thank you.' She wrapped her arms round his neck and covered him with kisses.

Even when she heard the office door opening, Thea didn't make a move to break away. It was only Dave's gentle but persistent coughing that finally caused the couple to pull apart.

'Is this some sort of research?' he

asked, grinning. 'I just came in with some good news for you. I thought you could take some time off. You deserve it. Take a week starting this Friday. Carry on.' Dave ambled out of the room chuckling.

'Let's go away, Thea. I'd like to organise a holiday for us.'

'Where shall we go?'

'How about I surprise you?'

Thea felt she'd had enough surprises for a lifetime, but this one she would enjoy. She held out her hand and looked at the beautiful ring Justin had placed on her finger. It was the third finger of her left hand, but Justin hadn't asked her to marry him even though he'd sort of hinted at it. 'Is this an engagement ring?' she blurted out.

'Would you like it to be?' countered Justin.

'Stop playing games, Justin Anderson. This isn't a film where we have to wait to the end to see if the handsome young man gets the girl.'

'The *beautiful* girl,' he elaborated,

grinning infuriatingly.

In spite of her frustration, Thea smiled back at him. 'I need to know what's happening, Justin. It's been such a tortuous journey, right from day one of meeting you to now. I need some clear direction, something simple and easy to follow.'

Justin nodded. 'You have put up with a lot since being around me, you deserve to be treated properly. I've a few business things to see to and you'll have loose ends to tie up. I'll get Toby to pick you up in the limo and bring you over to my place on Friday afternoon . . . if you're agreeable.'

There was nowhere she'd rather be than in the country with Justin. Plus she'd be able to drive her marvellous new car. 'That'll be the best holiday,' she sighed.

'We'll see,' he said, kissing her nose before dashing off.

It was only when she was alone in the office that Thea realised Justin hadn't answered her question. She was none the wiser as to whether he had proposed or not. Still, there was no denying that the ring was beautiful and so were the flowers. After a quick search, she found a chipped vase in the bottom of a cupboard, filled it with water and stuffed the bouquet into it.

* * *

When Toby picked her up at her flat after work on Friday, Thea was ready. Not wanting to be caught out again, she'd over-packed, but give him his due, Toby didn't raise an eyebrow as he lifted the two heavy cases into the boot of the limo.

'Won't be a minute,' called Thea, dashing back indoors. In seconds she reappeared clutching the flowers Justin had given her. 'You don't get hay fever, do you?' she enquired. 'I brought these back from the office so I'm not going to let them die at home now, they'll look lovely in Justin's kitchen.'

'Yes, Thea, they will.' Toby put a

hand on her shoulder. 'You're a breath of fresh air, you know that?'

Thea felt herself blushing and ducked quickly into the car. She sat in the front so that they could chat easily as she wanted to catch up on all the latest news of the family. 'Is this a new limo?'

'No, same old. I keep it garaged near my home which was a bit of luck as it was out of harm's way during the fire. It's the only car he's got left now from all those he had in his collection.'

'He didn't seem too bothered about losing the others.'

'Pretty sensible bloke, isn't he?' Toby quickly looked sideways and smiled. 'It's not my business, but Gracie has been pestering me to find out what's going on between you two.'

'How is she?' Thea changed the subject. 'It was lucky that environmental scandal came up just when we thought she was going to be exposed by the politician story. It didn't even make the headlines in the end.'

'Yeah, we breathed a sigh of relief. She's back at her flat, doing fine.'

'And how's Rae?'

'Still the same. You know Rae. So what do I tell Gracie?'

'Oh, I don't know.' Thea held out her hand and looked at the ring glittering in the sunshine.

'Sparkly. I'll tell her about that then.'

As they pulled into the drive Toby said, 'Before I get the cases out let's just walk. I want to show you something.' He led her to a new building.

'Oh, a proper garage, that was fast.'

'Justin wanted to get rid of all signs of the fire pretty quickly.' He unlocked the door and led Thea inside. 'There's your TVR. I was going to give it a wash down, but it's hardly been on the road.'

'We decided it's best if I keep it here, for the time being at least, as there isn't much point me having it in London *and* I've nowhere to park it.'

'And this is Justin's new vehicle.'

Thea squealed. 'A VW camper van. I've always imagined going on holiday in one of those. You know, with a surf board, camping by the beach. Is that what we're doing?'

'I'm saying nothing.' But Toby looked a little anxious.

* * *

Cruising on a restaurant boat on the Seine with Justin made the days Thea had spent at the office seem like a lifetime ago. Their day in Paris had been magical and they were still finding new things to marvel at. They'd just passed the Louvre and were making their way leisurely towards Notre Dame. Having enjoyed sea bream and braised vegetables they were now waiting for their dessert of citrus fruit savarin. The restaurant with its crisp white linen cloths and attentive staff was buzzing, but in spite of the people, Thea thought it was a charming place for lovers.

Justin reached across the table and took her hand. 'I fell for you the first time I saw you.'

'You mean when I was on the ground, having been knocked over by a bike?'

'Yes, it was love at first sight. You can't imagine how I felt when that awful woman sent me off so that I couldn't take you home. I thought I'd never see you again. I hoped you'd ring after I put my phone number in your bag.'

'But you haven't always shown your feelings. Sometimes I've wondered if you actually even liked me.'

'That's because I was scared. I was scared that you wouldn't feel the same. It's difficult for someone like me to face rejection when I've got so many women admiring me and falling at my feet. One of my many faults, I'm afraid. I was wondering if you'd be willing to put up with my imperfections full-time.'

'I think it may take me a little while to get used to them, but I might be prepared to give it a go.' Thea's tummy flipped. Had he just asked her to marry him?

As if in answer to her doubts, Justin got up swiftly and Thea wondered where he was going, but then he was in front of her, down on one knee, saying, 'Thea, I love you, will you do me the honour of marrying me?'

Thea stared at him silently until the other diners started laughing and urged her to answer the good-looking young man.

'I love you, too, Justin,' she said, 'and I'm glad that you've asked me to marry you.'

'This doesn't sound as if it's going to be as simple as I'd hoped,' sighed Justin. 'Come on, Thea, yes or no?'

'Can I think about it?' she asked, not quite sure why, except that so much had happened lately. 'I need some time to get my head around it. You're not the boy next door, you know, you're famous and you live in a different world . . . ' She looked around the group of people, but they'd lost interest now that there wasn't an apparently happy ending in sight.

'I know I'm asking a lot. Take all the time you need.' Justin jumped to his feet and called for another bottle of champagne.

★　★　★

'I can't believe it's Monday morning already,' Justin said, as he wolfed down a slice of toast. 'But it's great that we can travel in to work together. Toby should be here in ten minutes. Fancy a quick visit to see the animals? I would have gone last night, but it was too dark when we got back.'

Thea quickly put on her strawberry-red trainers, then holding hands they jogged to the animal enclosures. The pigs were looking fat and contented and were too busy snuffling in their trough to notice their visitors. In the horses' field there was more interest, especially as Justin had some pieces of carrot in his pocket. After munching them down, the animals wandered away. Thea felt deeply satisfied and nestled against

Justin, taking deep breaths of the fresh country air. Suddenly they were pushed apart from behind. Milly nudged herself between them, standing on Thea's trainers in the process. She didn't care one bit that her foot was being squashed and her trainers muddied. Thea and Justin patted Milly and she brayed contentedly.

'Don't tell anyone,' said Thea to Milly, 'but I'd like to be with you and Justin full-time. Will that be okay?'